you

P[...]e
Stone

Sam Bain

First published in 2002 by I.M.P. FICTION

This Edition © I.M.P. Fiction 2002
A catalogue record for this book is available
from The British Library

ISBN 0-9533275-6-6
1 2 3 4 5 6 7 8 9 10

Printed and bound in Great Britain.

Cover Designed by Phil Gambrill and I.M.P. Fiction.
Cover photograph by Paola De Grenet
With kind thanks to *Hello!* and *OK!* magazines.

I.M.P. Fiction Ltd
P. O. Box 14691, London, SE1 2ZA
Fax: 020 7357 8608   E-mail: info@impbooks.com

Visit I.M.P. FICTION at: *www.impbooks.com*

Yours Truly, Pierre Stone

by
Sam Bain

I.M.P. FICTION
London

ACKNOWLEDGEMENTS

Grateful thanks to Richard Francis and Michael
Schmidt, my teachers; Maggie Phillips, my agent;
Kaye Roach, my publisher; Jesse Armstrong, my compadre;
Philip Wells, my hero; and Rosie Bird, my angel.

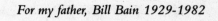

For my father, Bill Bain 1929-1982

Dear Miss Mitchell,

Sorry to interrupt your busy schedule. I know we've never met, but I felt I had to write to you. You must read things like this all the time, so I'd quite understand if you wanted to just throw it aside and forget about it.

My name is Pierre Stone and I'm one of your biggest fans. I'm writing to say how much I've been enjoying your appearances on *Decisions, Decisions* and *Ballroom Blitz*.

The first thing I'd like to say is, can you send me a photograph of yourself? A glamour snapshot would be fine, although I would prefer something of your own like a holiday photograph. That's probably very presumptuous, please forget I asked that. I know you are far too busy to get involved personally with queries such as mine.

Before I go, I'd like to say again how much pleasure I get out of your TV appearances. It's obvious that you take a great deal of trouble with the way you look, and the way you stand and speak. Your grace and charm far outweigh that of other people on TV and previous presenters of *Decisions, Decisions* like Claudia Carpenter. Although of course I don't want to be rude about Ms Carpenter. I just mean that your radiance is particularly special and meaningful to me.

Thank you for your time in reading this. I very much look forward to hearing from you and seeing you again on television. Best of luck with everything.

Yours truly,

Pierre Stone

PS: My mother just bought two tickets for the Christmas special.

Dear Miss Mitchell,

Hello again! You may not remember me, but my name is Pierre Stone and I wrote to you once before. I'm writing to say thank you so much for the photo you sent me, which I've had framed. I can't say what an honour it is for me to have something of yours in the house, although of course I would let you have it back if you needed it.

I've been very much enjoying the recent instalments of *Ballroom Blitz* and *Decisions, Decisions*, although I do feel that in the latter show Tony Clayton fails to give you enough respect as a performer and presenter. He seems to regard you merely as a pretty face, an attractive sidekick whom he can use to add some glamour to his tired image. I would prefer it if he gave you more authority. In fact, I would prefer it if he was your sidekick, and you took over, since most people only switch on to watch you.

I always record your programmes as I like to watch them each about three times. The first time, when the show is originally broadcast, is the best, because it's nice to know that millions of people are watching it at the exact same moment, including your family and friends. I don't like to be distracted when I'm watching, especially that first time, because I can't pause or rewind. So if my mother comes in to talk to me or fill the humidifier or whatever, then I do my best to ignore her.

At the beginning of the show, when Tony comes on to do his thing with the audience using his catchphrases and telling jokes, I feel a certain amount of tension and build-up, because I know you'll be appearing soon. When he introduces you and you come on, I have a rush of excitement and the reception you receive from the audience mirrors my own delight in having you onscreen.

From that point, I usually feel slightly disappointed because Tony, the contestants and the expert guests tend to dominate the show to such an extent. It's only at the end, when you and Tony dance a number together, that I feel he really lets you fulfil your potential. At that moment it must be clear to everyone that you far exceed him in terms of dancing skill and screen presence. Tony does his best to keep up, but really his performance is amateur when compared to your virtuosity.

This leads me on to the subject of *Ballroom Blitz* which I feel has a format that showcases your talent much more effectively. It really seems to be your show: there is no one there to question your authority or tell you what to do, and everyone in the audience knows of your expertise and respects you for it. It's obvious that you get real pleasure out of giving the dancers a chance to display their skills, and allowing the TV audience an opportunity to bear witness to the magical world of the ballroom.

The show also gives you a chance to dress up in gowns and dresses which otherwise you might never get to wear. Last week's edition was a good example; the scarlet silk of the dress perfectly contrasted with your silky complexion – a real "English Rose". I think your name, Marie Mitchell, is very suitable because it combines your traditional English qualities with the continental sophistication so necessary for the modern woman.

You'll be pleased to know that *Ballroom Blitz* actually inspired me to join a dance class in my local area. It was held on the first floor of an old town hall near where I live in Purley. There were about forty people there. Most of them came with a partner, and that made it easier for them to do a consistent amount of practice during the evening. At first everyone changed partners after each sequence of moves. All the men stood in one row and all the women stood opposite, and after every sequence we moved along one.

My first partner was a middle-aged lady, quite small, a sort of shrunken version of Madge from *Neighbours*. She had obviously done it before and was patient as I learned the moves and how to lead. My next partner was a younger girl, perhaps twenty-one, with long black hair and dungarees and a jaunty manner. She was much shorter than me, and that was the source of some amusement as we began to take up the Tango position. Eventually we got it right, with her left hand over my right shoulder, my right hand over her waist and our other hands meeting in a firm embrace.

When we had finished our dance, I gave her a smile. She responded with an awkward grin and unpeeled her fingers from mine before darting off to talk to a young unshaven man on the other side of the room. They obviously knew each other, but nevertheless I felt annoyed because she seemed to have no respect for the rules of the class, which clearly indicated that partners should be swapped in an ordered, formal manner.

After that, the class seemed less enjoyable. My next partner was a very tall, muscular woman of uncertain age who seemed to think that we were matched for the rest of the evening. I found it difficult to lead a person of such size and weight, and so made my excuses and took a seat on the edge of the hall. I noticed that she was forced to do the same as a result of my reluctance. After perhaps an hour of watching the other couples, I fetched my coat from the cloakroom and wandered home.

When I got home my mother was waiting, playing solitaire in the kitchen and smoking Silk Cut Ultra Lights. I barely had a chance to hang up my coat before she was up and jabbering at me with the same old questions:

"Did you have a nice time?"

"Would you like something to eat?"

"I've got some cakes in the bread bin," ... etc.

I pretended to listen while I fetched my carton of pineapple juice from the fridge. The shelf on our fridge door is rather narrow and tends to be quite full, so the cartons of fruit juice are usually stuffed tightly into it. I managed to wrestle it free and with a tug lifted up one of its corner wings. Then I crossed the kitchen, and made my way to the drawer which held the cutlery and metal implements. I opened it and selected the large Wilkinson Sword kitchen scissors with orange plastic handles.

The scissors were large and very sharp. I tensed the neck of the spout, and then sliced it off in one quick, clean movement. The opening was of a good size – big enough to let air in while the liquid was being poured, but not so large that any juice would be easily spilled.

After depositing the unneeded scrap of card in the dustbin, I went to reach for a glass before pausing and thinking. Maybe it would be better if I just went ahead and drank straight from the carton. I was very thirsty and the idea appealed to me. Of course, I knew that this was sure to result in some sort of complaint from my mother, but it was really none of her business. She was well aware that I was the sole consumer of pineapple juice in the house, so the only person receiving my germs at a later date would be myself.

I took firm hold of the box and lifted it to my lips. Then I stopped, mid-motion, as I heard my mother speak:

"Don't forget to shake it, dear."

I frowned. She was right, of course. Pineapple juice contains far more sediment than other fruit juices like apple or orange. For that reason you might think that she was making a perfectly innocent statement, issuing a simple piece of advice. But I knew that she had been waiting the whole time, watching, until the crucial moment when she could interrupt and cause me the maximum amount of frustration.

My choice was clear. I could carry on and risk wasting perhaps a fifth of my juice, which would be undrinkably thick with matter; or I could suffer the shame of backtracking and having my mother watch as I tried to shake the carton without spilling anything.

Well, I was thirsty. The pineapple juice was right there and I wanted it, so I drank it. When I had finished, I walked over and put it back in the fridge. I could feel my mother's eyes on me but I didn't look back, in fact I was trying to contain a smirk, which was becoming a giggle, which emerged as a laugh as I ran up the stairs and into my room.

After my excitement had subsided, I decided I would pluck up the courage to write to you. Later on that evening, after discarding many drafts, I finished and retired exhausted to bed.

That night I dreamt vividly about you. In the dream, I was standing outside a cashpoint on the main road. I went to put my card in the slot, but it snapped in two. Then I heard a honk on a car horn, and I turned round to see you in the back seat of a Honda Civic with Michelle from *EastEnders*. In the front was Chris Packham who presents *The Really Wild Show* on Children's BBC. For some reason, he was incredibly fat and had to sit across both seats to drive the car.

You called me over, smiling, and I bent down to hear what you had to say. But every time you started to speak, Chris would rev up the engine very loud so I couldn't make out a single word. I got annoyed and shouted at him to stop, but then he just drove off, and through the open window I could hear you and Michelle laughing.

That's all I have time for now. Thank you for reading this.

Yours truly,

Pierre Stone

Dear Marie,

How are you? It's your friend Pierre Stone back again. I hope you are well and in good shape. I'm sorry to disturb you, but I just thought I'd write to see how you are and to tell you a bit about how I've been getting on.

I woke up a ten o'clock today, so I could lie in without missing the whole morning. I rolled out of bed feet first and my slippers were right there, my dressing gown was right there, on a hook, so I went straight out and into the bathroom. When I got into the bathroom, I turned two shower taps on first, because I wanted just the right blend of hot and cold so I wouldn't burn or freeze myself. I use coloured tape to indicate exactly the right place to have the cold tap once the hot tap is on full.

When I'm in the shower I wash myself the way a doctor does. This is how: first, take the soap and lather up, then put it back on the stand. Now you have lathered hands and you must use them one by one to wash each other. Extend your left hand and grasp the palm with your right hand. Then move this hand over your fingers and up over your thumb like a ski-jump. Do this process vigorously, then exchange hands. If you want to do it really fast, you can pretend you're in a competition to be the best doctor in the world.

After I finished in the bathroom, I got dressed and went downstairs to the kitchen. My mother had left a note on the table saying that she was out shopping till lunch. I breathed a sigh of relief and decided to go to the newsagent to get some things.

The newsagent is also a foodstore and a confectionery – in most respects a corner shop, except that it's not on a corner. My mother has always said that it's a bad idea to buy food and sweets from a corner shop, because they're more expensive than in the supermarket. But it really is the only local shop with such a wide range of magazines and chocolates, so I don't feel wrong to go there.

When you go in, on your right are the shelves of magazines, five rows of them, with newspapers and newsprint periodicals like *Exchange & Mart* at the bottom. The next row stocks mainly computer magazines and children's magazines. The third row contains women's magazines, beauty magazines and suchlike. There are so many of those that they spill over into the next row, which also has music magazines and sports magazines. The top row has fitness magazines and other magazines.

On the opposite side to that is the sweet stand, which backs on to the cashier's area. Beneath the racks of chocolate bars are large baskets which contain packets of crisps: Walkers, Quavers, Hula Hoops, Monster Munch etc. Usually my favourites are Cheese and Onion Walkers, Original Hula Hoops or Roast Beef Monster Munch which have the tall purple monster on the front. But today I wasn't interested in crisps – I wanted some chocolate, and I spent some minutes trying to decide what to choose.

I've gone through various phases in my taste in chocolate. The first chocolate bar I can remember liking was Curly Wurly. I think it was the curly shape that appealed to me, and the way that the toffee would stretch out when you took a bite, and fragments of chocolate coating would come too, like bits of broken shell.

At primary school, chocolate bars became much more important because of packed lunches. Everyone would compare what food they had. My mother would always give me the most, like a whole Mars bar, when Lawrence Wu and everyone else only got mini ones. At first that was the source of some status for me, but later it went sour and everyone got jealous and thought I was spoiled.

Later, when I changed school after my father died, everyone had hot lunches served by the school canteen, but my mother didn't want me eating that food so I still got packed lunches. Sometimes I sat with the teachers because the other children weren't very nice.

I went off Mars bars after a while, although I still like the way that when you bite into them the caramel breaks up through the chocolate, and it looks like a volcanic eruption on the planet Mars. After Mars bars I went through Twix, Marathon, Star Bar, Boost, Cabana, Caramel, Finger of Fudge, Galaxy, Dairy Crunch, Bar Six, Whole Nut Yorkie and all the rest, apart from Kit Kat which I've never liked, and mints, which I hate.

After various scans along the display, I still couldn't make up my mind, so I plumped for Toffee Crisp, which is my recent favourite. I picked up a copy of *Hello!* and *Radio Times*, and went round to the till to pay. I had noticed that it was the manager of the shop serving, not his young female assistant, which was slightly disappointing but also made me feel more relaxed.

When I got home, I made a cup of tea and opened up my copy of *Hello!*. The centre spread was a photo-article on Olivia Newton-John and her husband Matt. Olivia is looking radiantly healthy after her cancer treatment, especially after a few months in her beloved Australia. And now she and Matt, who's an actor, have moved into their dream house, an environmentally-friendly mansion clinging to the rocks above the sea, but still in Malibu. The house means a fresh start after the trials of the past two years, and is exactly what they wanted because Matt helped design and build it. Beauty and practicality are combined in the lovely kitchen with its adjoining dining area. The pool has a built-in current simulator, and like the rest of the house, captures the maximum amount of light.

I was impressed by the house and pleasantly surprised by how well Olivia was looking after her terrible ordeal. Like most people, I still have fond memories of her in *Grease* and her beauty seems hardly to have dimmed. Matt seemed all right, although his hair looked quite thin in some of the photos.

Other parts of the magazine included a day in the life of Claudia Schiffer, the supermodel, and the actress Susan George at home with her husband Simon MacCorkindale, whom you may remember from the TV series *Manimal*.

After that, my mother came home from shopping and I had to help her unload the car, which I'm sure you wouldn't want to hear about.

Before I forget, I had another dream about you, which is actually what inspired me to write.

In the dream I was sitting on a park bench next to you. I was looking at you and I couldn't move my head. You were very energetic – you kept wriggling in your seat and then you leapt off the bench and ran around the park. After you ran off, I noticed that sitting on the other side of you was Fred Dineage, who used to present the TV programme *How!*, only he was wearing a gangster's outfit with a fedora and a pencil moustache. He didn't look at me, he looked straight ahead, and he was telling me about some scheme he had hatched to get to the airport or something. He was talking about all the video games they had there.

I looked past him, into the distance, and noticed two figures on a hill above a lake. I looked closer and realized it was Melvyn Bragg from *The South Bank Show*, and Richard Stilgoe, who used to present *Finders Keepers* and also wrote the lyrics for *Starlight Express*. They were wearing Morris Dancers' costumes and were dancing around on the top of the hill, occasionally linking their arms at the elbow and cavorting in circles around each other.

I shifted focus to look back at Fred Dineage, but for some reason he had changed into Jonathan Cohen, who used to play the piano and join in the songs on *Playaway*. He was wearing exactly the same costume and was still talking about the same thing, ie, how to get to the airport and all the video games.

I looked away again, this time towards the lake. It was night time there, despite the fact that it was broad daylight everywhere else. Around the edge of the lake there were a lot of fat, overdressed, over-made-up Italian women drinking cocktails and apparently having a party. You were there in your red dress and it seemed as though they were having the party for you.

I still couldn't move my head, in fact I was immobile, stuck in the same position, with my left leg bent under my right knee, and my hands sandwiched between my thighs. Then Jonathan Cohen – who had now become John Craven, presenter of

Newsround – turned to me, very agitated, saying:

"You don't want to come to the airport, do you? You never wanted to come to the airport! You never wanted to come at all!"

He kept repeating this over and over again, and I still couldn't move, and then I woke up. The dream was pretty disturbing but on the whole I was pleased it had happened. I wonder if you have any idea what it means?

Yours truly,

Pierre Stone

Dear Marie,

Today was not a fantastic day for your friend. Today I went to get a job – not because I particularly wanted one, but because of the agreement I have with my mother, which is that I should get a job.

The only job I've had up to now is working at home as an assistant to my mum. In that job I had various tasks, eg, make the bed, clear up the room, hoover the landing, fold the towel properly, clean your fingernails and put the breakfast things in the dishwasher. It was OK, although I wasn't that good at it. Making the bed I found particularly difficult. My bed is right next to the wall, it's in the corner of my room in fact, and so trying to tuck the sheets under the mattress on that side is really very hard (not to mention the blankets, which are thicker). Also, I don't like folding up the towel. When I've finished washing my hands I just want to dry them quickly and then leave to do something else. I don't want to hang around folding the towel for ages.

Hoovering was probably my favourite part of the job, but it tends to be over quite quickly and then you have to do something more difficult. Also, if I couldn't do something very well, like making the bed for example, I would lounge around feeling sorry for myself, which doesn't get anyone anywhere. I think that's one of the reasons I got sacked from that job.

Still, I'd been doing it for a few years and except for the odd problem which I mentioned above, I had got quite used to it. If I was doing jobs in my room and my mother was busy elsewhere in the house or she was out having the car serviced, then I could stay there and read. Apart from magazines like *Hello!*, *Radio Times*, *TV Times* and *Smash Hits!*, I have books which I occasionally look at. At the moment I am reading a story about a young knight whose princess is trapped by a dragon at the top of a glass mountain. The mountain is so smooth and sheer that the only way the knight can climb it is by using two bear's paws to claw his way up. At night he must sleep clinging on to the paws, with no protection from the bitterly cold wind which slices through his thin shirt. I'll tell you the rest of the story later.

I might as well give you some more details about my bedroom since you're probably finding it hard to visualize. The first thing you'd notice when you came in is all the pictures on the walls, of which there are many. I would point out to you first the signed photograph of yourself which stands in pride of place on my bedside table. As you can see I've had it framed in a brass frame which I bought from a shop down the road.

Then you might want to turn your attention to the wall opposite my bed which is filled with *Smash Hits!* Pop Profiles and Pin-Ups. I have a wide assortment which is constantly being updated. It includes older bands such as Tight Fit and Modern Romance, as well as new ones like Take That and Bad Boys Inc. The Pin-Ups are just colourful photographs of singers and band members, and those get changed most often because they can become boring. However, the Pop Profiles include questionnaires answered by all the individual members of the band, and those are much more interesting. For example, 3 out of 5 members of Duran Duran say that their favourite food is hot buttered toast.

The next wall is the window wall, ie, it is mainly glass and has no pictures, except I suppose the garden, which you can see if you look through it. The third wall, which is the wall on which my head rests when I read in bed, is decorated with posters of various heroes. First we have the Thundercats, who consist of Tigra, Cheetara, Panthro and Lion-O, the leader. They fight a never-ending war against the evil wizard Mumm-Ra on a distant planet. Next there is a poster from the TV series *The Incredible Hulk* starring Lou Ferrigno as the angry green man who overturns trucks. Also on this wall there are pictures of Evel Knievel, the Man from Atlantis, Poncherello from CHiPs, and Michael Knight, the man who does not exist.

The final wall is my celebrity wall and that is covered in

a celebrity collage. Think of it as a web with yourself at the centre, because there you are, in the middle, in a picture I cut out from *Radio Times*. On what you might call the 'inner circle' of the web, are pictures of those celebrities whom you probably get along with best: Janet Ellis, Michaela Strachan, Anthea Turner, Ulrika Jonsson, Caron Keating and Carol Vorderman, who helps present *Countdown*. Also in the 'inner circle' are those celebrity ladies who would best act as your bodyguards: the more athletic types like Cheryl Ladd, Jaclyn Smith and Tanya Roberts from *Charlie's Angels* as well as Lindsay Wagner from *The Bionic Woman* and Jet from *Gladiators*.

Then, on the next ring, are those celebrities whom you turn to for advice if ever you need it. They include *Mastermind* host Magnus Magnusson, along with Barry Norman, Norris McWhirter, Patrick Moore, Tony Hart and Magnus Pyke. On the third ring we have the 'court jesters' like Ken Dodd, Bobby Ball and Freddie Starr.

The fourth ring is made up of more general servants. There are the cooks – Delia Smith, Ken Hom and Rusty Lee; the wine tasters, Oz Clarke and Jilly Goolden; the butler, Gordon Jackson; the personal trainer, Rosemary Conley; and Barry Sheen, who acts as both chauffeur and emergency despatch rider, despite the pins in his leg. Not to mention your tennis partner, Virginia Wade, your judo coach, Brian Jacks, or your Scrabble partner, Paul Coia. The Gladiators, led by Wolf, are your palace guards, and they strive to protect you from any attack.

In the palace you take things at your leisure. You wake at whatever hour you please in your terrific four-poster bed, curled up in sheets which are changed regularly. Sometimes when you wake, beautiful cartoon birds surround your head and sing like in *Snow White*. Also on occasion you will have had a pyjama party or a midnight feast with some of your friends, and a few may be asleep in your bed. For example, if Ulrika Jonsson and Anthea Turner are asleep beside you, you will be careful not to wake them as you creep out of bed and into the shower, cautiously avoiding the Cluedo and Monopoly sets strewn across the floor.

Perhaps in days of old, you would have had ladies-in-waiting to bathe and clothe you, but this is the modern world, and you move with the times and expect high performance. The soap you use is Dove Cream Bar, which has a neutral pH and contains 25% moisturizer. The toothpaste you use is Ultra Brite, which you dispense onto a Reach toothbrush, one with a bendy head which gets right in there, behind your teeth and into your gums. Being well aware that tooth brushing functions primarily to fight gum disease rather than tooth decay, you make sure that you brush in small circles at an angle towards your gums. Also, you take at least three whole minutes to brush your teeth slowly and carefully, both back and front. You don't just zoom around and scrub out the bits of nut and crisp, you take your time and do it well and your teeth are all the better for it.

After showering, you wrap yourself in your thick Marks and Spencer dressing gown and moccasin slippers before tiptoeing past your dozing friends. On the way, you stop and peer over to check they are all right. You smile at the sight of Anthea's hand resting gently on the brushed cotton shoulder of Ulrika's nightgown.

Once out of your room, you enter the landing-stroke-balcony which overlooks the hall downstairs and leads on to the huge central staircase, a bit like Scarlett O'Hara's in *Gone With The Wind*. On the wall are large and impressive portraits of absent friends and former house guests, such as Bob Monkhouse, Sandra Dickinson and Ray Reardon. You greet Jet (the Gladiator) and Cheryl Ladd, who have been standing guard outside your room all night and are now resting on camp stools, sharing tea from a Thermos flask.

Instead of taking the stairs you step into a large basket strewn with flowers which hangs suspended from the balcony, and you are winched slowly to the ground by Jet and Cheryl. Once downstairs, you enter the spacious and beautifully fitted kitchen to see Carol Vorderman at the mahogany table, eating the last of a packet of Crunchy Nut Corn Flakes. Carol looks up and begins to apologize for having finished off the cereal, but you silence her with a smile.

You then turn to a cupboard and open it to reveal a shelf full of assorted cereals, including Coco Pops, Rice Krispies, Shreddies, Weetabix, Nut Feast, Ricicles, and Kellogg's Special K. Taking down an unopened box of Special K, you sit at the table where bowls, spoons and a jug of semi-skimmed milk have been prepared for you by Gordon Jackson. You take care to read the back of the cereal packet first, considering any recipes or special offers. Then you open it, in a swift motion which leaves the top untorn, and quickly search for the secret prize, be it a colourful dinosaur or miniature car. After that you are free to start your day, but first you calculate how much more Riboflavin, Niacin and Vitamin B12 you will have to eat for your recommended daily intake.

I should also mention that if the weather warrants it, you choose an alternative means of descent to the ground floor, via the spiral waterslide which extends from your bedroom window to the outdoor pool below.

Sorry, I had to break off there for a minute because my mother called me to have dinner. As it's Monday today, we had sausages and mash, and I ate it as fast as possible. I burnt my tongue a little on a sausage but I quickly washed it down with some apple juice so my mother wouldn't notice. Anyway, I'm forgetting what you wanted to hear about in the first place, which is my job-hunting. In order to do it, my mother drove me to our local orange building, the Jobcentre. Inside they have lists of jobs which are available for people to do. These are printed onto small cards which are fixed to the walls in rows, in categories like Cleaning, Typing, Cooking and Driving.

My mother explained to me that it was a waste of time to apply for a job I couldn't do, like driving or typing. Then she took me over to a sign which explained that when I saw a job I thought I might like, I should take the card from the wall, write down the number of the card on a piece of paper along with my name, and take it to one of the people behind the desks. Then she said she had to go and do some shopping on the High Street, and would I be all right till she got back.

I said yes because I could tell it was the answer she wanted, but once she was outside I looked again at the wall of cards and I didn't know what to do. It was like trying to choose chocolate but much harder. I ran out of the shop and down the street to where I could see her and asked her to come back and help me.

I could tell she was a little bit annoyed but I knew she wouldn't mind that much. We went back to the shop and started again to choose the card I wanted. We talked about what I could do and what I would like to do, and eventually we agreed that we should build on my skills with the hoover and apply for a job which involved some cleaning. Taking down the details from a card which spoke of employment as a part-time office cleaner for 13 hours a week, we went to talk to one of the desk people.

When I handed the man my piece of paper, he punched a few buttons on his computer and read out a description of the job I had decided to do. Then he glanced up at my mother, and she glanced towards me. He asked me if I had ever done this kind of work before. I said I had, he said in what capacity, I said just around the house. At that point he paused and gave my mother a rather searching look. She responded with a moment's silence before blurting out an embarrassing speech about what a good boy I was despite the fact that I hadn't had any real paid work experience and that I just needed a part-time job, something simple, just to help pay the bills. The man looked back at me and I raised my eyebrows and gave him a "Mothers, you know," sort of expression, because I could tell we had developed an understanding and I didn't want my mother to spoil it.

At that point he looked slightly unsettled but nevertheless went ahead and picked up the phone to call the person who had advertised the job. I was expecting him to pass the phone to me so I could introduce myself, but he didn't, and instead told the man on the other end that I had no experience. The conversation didn't last very long after that. He replaced the receiver, turned to me with a trace of a smile and told me that the 'employer' was looking for someone with a few more qualifications.

I turned to my mum but she just sat there with a rather pained expression on her face. My stomach began to churn and my face was going red. Why hadn't I been given the chance to get this job which I could probably do quite well? It seemed horribly unfair to advertise jobs to people and then lie and not let them have a chance. I began to frown, I felt my lip curl and my eyes were starting to sting. I looked at the man who I thought was my friend with his smug black face and I wanted to spit in his eye, or do something. But I didn't want to give him the satisfaction.

We left right after that, and on the drive home there wasn't much conversation between us. I suppose there wasn't that much to say.

Wishing you all the best as usual,

Pierre Stone

PS: The knight climbs the mountain, kills the dragon and marries the princess.

Dear Marie,

Sorry it's been so long since I last wrote, but I've been quite busy. Yesterday (Wednesday) my mother dropped me off at at car boot sale in nearby Coulsdon. I must admit that I'm a fan of second–hand shops, jumble sales and car boot sales. It's amazing what you can find in those places. In the past few months I've bought everything from an original James Bond Aston Martin, complete with revolving number–plates and an ejector seat, to a comic book featuring Superman vs Muhammad Ali (Superman won).

When my mother dropped me off at the sale, I was pretty excited by the thought of what sort of bargains I could pick up. My instincts led me straight to the record stall, and I started leafing through the boxes of old albums and singles in earnest. I didn't come across much in the way of real finds, apart from an old Shakatak single I'd been looking for and the soundtrack album for *Silver Dream Racer* starring David Essex which I also picked up. I contemplated buying 'Snooker Loopy' by Chas 'n' Dave but decided against it.

Putting the records into a large size carrier bag I had brought especially, I zipped up my anorak tighter, as there was a real nip in the air. I put the change from my purchase in the money pocket of my trousers, which is the most secure. I was wearing the trousers I always wear when I go out to jumble sales, which have many different pockets for many different functions. They are made of grey canvas with elastic round the ankle and a popper which fastens round the waist. There are six pockets: the normal two back pockets and two front pockets, as well as a zip pocket over the right knee and a smaller pocket with a flap just above the left. I keep my money in the former and my keys in the latter, since they are the most secure. The other pockets contain less interesting things such as handkerchiefs and leaflets.

After the record stall, I went over to the book stall, not really to look for books but instead to greet the lady who runs it, who once offered me a cup of soup. However, when I got there I saw that she was busy having an argument with her husband who also runs the stall, and I thought it best not to disturb her. Instead I had a look through the books in the box in front of me. One in particular caught my eye: it was the 1978 *Starsky And Hutch* BBC TV Annual. I opened it and looked inside. There were lots of pictures and illustrations of the TV police duo in various action poses, and in the centre pages there was an article about their favourite foods. These are their menus of choice:

STARSKY	*HUTCH*
Prawn Cocktail	Natural Yoghurt with Sea Kelp
★	★
Sausages in Beer	Stuffed Green Peppers
★	★
Pancakes with Maple Syrup	Fruit Salad

As you can see, Starsky is an omnivore, whereas Hutch is very much a vegetarian. He learned most of his recipes from his mother, Mrs Hutchinson.

I decided to postpone buying the book until the woman had finished her argument, and I put it back in the box. Then I wandered around for a while, eventually finding myself in a jewellery and second-hand clothes stall, which I hadn't seen before. I was just browsing around when the girl behind the jewellery counter said something. I wasn't sure what she said or whether she was addressing me, so I looked up, and she said it again. She called me 'love' and asked me if I was looking for a present for 'someone special'.

I was surprised by what she said and realized at once that she was an outgoing person. She was about thirty, but trying hard to look twenty-one, with too much make-up and dyed black hair. She was wearing a fake fur coat with a black T-shirt, a crucifix and black leather trousers. She was chewing gum and looking at me with a 'cheeky' expression.

"Actually I am," I replied. I thought that would surprise her.

She asked what this person was like.

"Well for a start," I continued, trying to suppress a smile, "she's a dancer. Also she works in television."

I must admit I felt an odd sort of thrill, talking about you to a perfect stranger who didn't have the faintest clue that the person being discussed was one of Britain's biggest stars. She showed me a few pairs of earrings, and then she reached down to the front of the display to fetch a necklace for me to look at. Her T-shirt was quite loose and she wasn't wearing a bra, so I was confronted with the sight of her pale chest and cleavage.

I glanced down her T-shirt and then I looked at her all over. The white make-up on her face was so thick that it looked like paint, and she had used eyeliner to draw a line at the corner of each eye, which looked amateur and ugly. She was very thin and her leather trousers were very tight around her hips. I realized that she was bending over like this on purpose to flirt with me.

I felt a strong need to escape from this sordid situation, and I decided that the best course of action would be to get out of the stall as quickly as possible. Making some mumbled excuses, I left, and looked round a couple more stalls before departing the market altogether. I was still a bit shaken by my experience, and I felt some regret at having mentioned you to that sort of woman, because I don't want our relationship degraded.

I set off for the bus-stop and called in on a newsagent on the way, so I could buy some chocolate and calm my nerves. I chose a bar of Golden Cup, and as I waited for my change at the till, I puzzled over the video playing on the black and white television high on the wall in front of me. From the scene I was watching, which lasted a very long time, it seemed to be a film about a man stacking shelves and pricing things. I stayed there, waiting to see what would happen, until I began to get in the way of the other customers, and I left to resume my walk to the bus-stop.

As I opened the bar of chocolate I remembered that I had forgotten to buy that *Starsky And Hutch* Annual, but it was too late to go back. It was getting dark, and I realized it was school-leaving time when I saw a crowd of schoolchildren at the bus shelter. Most of them were from the secondary school down the road and their uniforms were rather shabby. A lot of the boys were wearing trainers and some of the girls were wearing make-up and jewellery. I stood next to two quite young girls who were playing a 'pat-a-cake' sort of game, surprisingly to the tune of 'That's The Way I Like It' by KC And The Sunshine Band. I don't know if you know the song, but it goes: "That's the way, Uh-Huh Uh-Huh, I like it, Uh-Huh Uh-Huh."

A bus came and most of the people at the bus-stop got on, including the two girls, still playing 'pat-a-cake'. The only people left were myself, an old lady and a group of teenage boys. The boys were talking amongst themselves, and then I noticed from the corner of my eye that they were looking at me and lowering their voices. I just kept looking out towards the direction the bus would come from and thrust my hands deep into my pockets. After a while, I heard one of them approach me from my left and speak.

"Hey mister, have you got ten pee for the phone?"

I knew he was talking to me but I decided that the best thing to do would be to ignore him and hope the bus arrived soon. I heard more whispering noises and also some giggles, and then another voice, addressing me from the same side.

"Hey mister, have you got ten pee for the phone?"

Again I refused to humour them with a response because it was clear that they were only trying to taunt me. I just pretended that I hadn't heard.

"Oi mister, my mate asked you something."

This new voice was older, more aggressive, and I began to feel scared. My cheeks were going red and I was beginning to sweat, but I thought that if I hadn't answered them before, I couldn't start now. Then I heard more laughter and felt the voices coming nearer.

"Yeah mister, answer him."

"Go on, give us ten pee."

"He just needs it to phone his mum."

"Don't you want to talk to us?"

"We just want to be your friend, mister."

"Yeah, go on, just give us ten pee."

By now they were all around me, the voices coming from all sides. Some of them were in front of me, looking me straight in the eye. I felt a rising wave of panic and it was obvious that I couldn't go on ignoring them much longer. I didn't look at any of them but instead my hand went down to the zip of my money pocket.

"If I give you ten pee will you leave me alone?"

There was a moment's silence as my voice cut through theirs. I was trembling, the zip wouldn't open, I wanted them all to go away and I very much wanted the bus to come. I finally got out the ten pee and then it started, the laughter, like a wave crashing over me. I held out the ten pee in my hand but they didn't want it, they were just looking for an excuse to laugh at me. Suddenly I saw the bus coming. I flagged it down, got on, paid my fare and ran upstairs. I was very lucky that they didn't get on the same bus. I managed to calm down a bit, and when I got home my mother made me fish and chips with peas and I went to bed early.

Yours truly,

Pierre Stone

Dear Marie,

How are you? I hope you are well. It's nice to be talking to you again like this. Of course, I've been watching all the episodes of *Decisions, Decisions* and enjoying them very much. I hope you have been enjoying them as much as me, although you probably have your mind on other projects such as the new series of *Ballroom Blitz* (I hope) and the pantomime in Birmingham. I read about it in the local paper and I'm already trying to persuade my mother to get some tickets. With a cast that includes Lesley Judd, Stu Francis, Linda Lusardi and Sooty, it could hardly be anything but a big success.

You may remember from my letter last week that I made a deal with my mother about getting a job. I had hoped she would forget about it but she didn't, and for a few days we argued about me going back to the Jobcentre. Eventually I managed to persuade her that there was no point going because all the jobs would have been taken, but she still insisted that I kept my word. She said that she didn't want to make me miserable, but that I should learn to stand on my own two feet because she wouldn't always be around to help me.

So this afternoon after lunch I set off to ask for work in the local shops. I could have started yesterday, but I wanted a day to prepare and also today is Tuesday, which is a good day. There are only two days in the week which aren't good, Monday and Wednesday. Monday because it's the very first weekday, and Wednesday because it's right in the middle of the week. Saturday is my favourite day because that's when *Decisions, Decisions* is on. Friday is a good day because it's at the end of the week and there's Saturday to look forward to. Thursday is fun because it's right before Friday, and I like Tuesday because it begins with the same letter as Thursday, which is a fun day, as I mentioned above.

I started my job-hunt on Brighton Road, which is the nearest main road to where we live. First I thought I'd go to Costcutter, where I buy my sweets and magazines. The manager was there but he was serving a customer, and while he did so I flicked through the magazine rack. I had a look at girls' magazines which I would never normally buy, such as *Just Seventeen*, *More!*, *Top Santé* and *Prima*. I found out some interesting things. For example, Melissa Gilbert from *Little House On The Prairie* is set to wed Bruce Boxleitner, whom you may remember from *Scarecrow And Mrs King*. Also, you might not think mumsy Gloria Hunniford and off-beat singer Suzanne Vega have anything in common – but you'd be wrong. In their younger days, they both worked as an Avon Lady, selling cosmetics door to door.

Eventually, after I'd looked through all the girls' magazines, pop magazines and women's magazines, I went over to the till. I waited for a few seconds before the manager saw me and put down his paper.

"Do you have any... jobs, going, at the moment?" I asked.

"Sorry, do I have any what?" he said, bending towards me.

"Um, I said, do you have any... chocolate?"

He frowned.

"No you didn't. You said something about 'Yops'."

"No, I said... I meant to say, 'Do you have any chocolate..?' Chocs!"

"What?"

"What I said was, 'Do you have any chocs?' Meaning chocolate. Do you have any chocs?"

He was silent for a moment.

"Of course we've got bloody chocolate. You buy some almost every day."

"Yes, well, I just wanted to make sure that nothing had changed. Thanks very much!" I said, making my way towards the door.

I was pleased to be out of the shop but I hoped the manager wasn't too angry with me and would let me back in there again. My first thought was to go straight back home and plead with my mum, but I knew she would be upset if I did that. I decided that I had to try again.

Over the road from Costcutter is the Midland Pub, and I thought I might look in there, since I've never been in before and consequently nobody knows me. The front double doors were quite heavy, but I pushed them open and went in. There were only a few people inside: two girls behind the bar, two men playing pool and another, older man sitting by himself with a pint of beer. It was a very spacious pub and I felt quite conspicuous coming in on my own. Just ahead of me I could see a pinball machine which was called *I, Robot*. I went up to it and had a closer look. The screen above the table showed a huge metal robot woman reclining on the surface of a planet, with lots of little men in space suits standing on cranes and welding her. I fished out a fifty pee piece from my pocket and put it in the slot. The machine made a strangely attractive laughing sound and I moved closer, placing my hands on either side, with my fingers poised over the buttons.

I examined the table itself. It seemed that the aim of the game was to bring to life the robot-woman. To do so, one had to shoot the ball up a ramp and into her mouth, which was a wide open hole at the end of the table. This would give her the power of speech, and then one had to shoot into her eyes to make her see and into her brain to make her think.

I pressed Start, and then released the spring-loaded stick to propel the ball up the launch tunnel. It flew up the table and then began to wend its way back toward me, ricocheting off various targets and buffers. When it reached my right-hand flipper, I hit the button and sent it through a spinning gateway, lodging it in a high-scoring prize bunker. After a few seconds the ball was ejected into the channel leading to my left flipper. I watched its progress, and waited for the exact moment when it reached the very end of the flipper. Then I hit the button hard. The ball streaked upwards and came to rest, falling neatly into the she-robot's mouth.

At that moment the machine seemed as though it had woken up - lights flashed, numbers raced across the scoreboard and then the sound of a female voice came floating towards me.

"I... Can... Speak..." it said.

My heart glowed.

Then, to my horror, the ball was roughly ejected from her mouth and left to trickle down a metal gutter towards me. It arrived in the channel leading to my right flipper, but I was so unprepared that I failed to hit it in time, and could only watch in dismay as it slipped past and was lost in the void between my flippers.

Looking up at where I had entered her mouth, I noticed that where the mouth-hole had been, there was now a face with two vacant eyes, staring at me. Another ball appeared in the launch tunnel. After a moment's hesitation I shot it upwards, saw it come down and then hit it with my flipper, missing her face but striking a target marked Lungs for 2,000 extra points. It stayed there for a couple of seconds and then shot out towards me, but so fast that I didn't have time to respond. I could only watch helplessly as the ball dived directly between my flippers and into oblivion.

Another ball appeared in the tunnel. I checked her eyes for any trace of expression, but they were vacant as before. I decided to ignore the disappointment of losing my last ball so quickly, and released the stick. The ball banged back and forth on the board and then sped down towards me. I caught it with the right flipper, and then sent it over to the left, bouncing it left and right until eventually I lost control and saw it follow the others into the void. I remained motionless for a second, and glanced up at the scoreboard: Game Over. As I turned away from the table, I heard the bubbling sound of electronic laughter, mocking me, ringing in my ears as I stormed out of the pub and into the street.

I decided that I had to put a stop to these constant attacks on my pride. I had looked for a job in two places and my mother was sure to understand that I had tried and failed. There was nothing bad about that. I would simply go home and explain that there were no jobs available that day.

I walked quickly home only to find that my mother was out. She had left a note on the kitchen table which said: "At the hairdressers until 2:30." Underneath the note was a tea towel which covered my lunch: cold roast chicken with a salad and bread rolls to bake in a preheated oven for 10 minutes at gas mark 6. I poured myself some apple juice, which she'd forgotten, put it all on a tray and carried it into the front room. It was 13:19 by the Ceefax clock, so I had time to eat it all before *Neighbours* and *XYZ* with George Marshall. On *XYZ* there was a question asking which *Decisions, Decisions* hostess Tony Clayton married – Georgette Peters of course. The question reminded me of you, so after the programme I wrote you this letter. I hope you've enjoyed it.

Yours truly,

Pierre Stone

Dear Marie,

In my last letter I told you about my activities on Tuesday, and my attempts to find work. When my mother came home I told her about it as well, and she was sympathetic. However, she insisted that I try again to get a job. I didn't want to, and I tried to protest, but she got so upset that I had to agree. She told me that I had to face it sooner or later, and that it might as well be sooner. I could tell she meant it. So at about 3 o'clock today, I found myself again walking down Brighton Road, this time towards Foxley Lane.

The first shop I came to was a hardware and key-cutting shop. I knew there was no point asking in there, since to do so I would have to know something about hardware and/or keys. The next shop was the butcher's, and I looked in the window at the men chopping up joints of meat and weighing pounds of mince. It didn't take long for me to realize that this was also something that I wasn't qualified to do.

After going past what seemed like hundreds of shops, all unsuitable, I came across Portofino, our local Italian restaurant. I looked at the window and immediately saw a sign: "Help Wanted - Waiter/Waitress Needed To Start ASAP." I stopped to think. This was another job which I had no experience of or qualifications for, but the handwriting seemed nice and I remembered the restaurant from having gone there with my mother for a birthday treat. She had asked for a birthday cake to be brought out as a surprise. The staff sang 'Happy Birthday', and afterwards the manager came up and shook my hand and offered me many happy returns.

I decided that today would be a good chance to accept his offer, so I pushed open the door and went inside. There were only a couple of customers in the restaurant. I looked around and then saw a man at the bar, who I recognized as being the manager. I decided that the best thing to do would be to go up to him at once and announce my intentions.

"Hello," I said, striding towards him. "You may not remember me, but I've come for the job in the window."

He took a moment to collect his thoughts, and then said that I'd come at a good time, as they weren't very busy at that moment.

"Yes," I said. "When I had that birthday meal here it was quite full."

He invited me to sit down, and gestured to a nearby table, at which we both proceeded to sit. He told me that as it wasn't a huge place, he only had two waiters working at any one time, and they were expected to pretty much look after themselves. Then he asked me if I'd had any experience.

"Not really," I said. "But I'm willing to learn."

He leaned back in his chair. He said that he wanted to be honest with me, and that he was looking for someone with a little more experience.

"Please," I said. I could feel my heart beating faster. "I can learn – I'm a fast learner, and I really like being polite and friendly to people. I don't care what you pay me, I'll work for nothing, I don't mind, I just really need a job. Please."

He opened his mouth slightly. "You'll work for nothing?"

"Yes, I'd love to. Just please give me the chance. I just need a chance. Please?"

He looked at me and frowned. He said he wouldn't normally do this, but he did need someone for the lunchtime shift tomorrow. He said he wasn't making any promises, and that Karina would be there to help me, but if I wanted I could come in at 11.

"Great! Thank you. Thank you so much. I won't let you down."

He gave me a form to fill in and told me what to wear – black trousers, black shoes and a T-shirt. I wondered whether the restaurant might have more customers if the staff dressed more cheerfully, but I didn't say anything, apart from "Yes" and "Thanks again."

The whole thing was much easier than I had expected. I was pleased that I had made the effort because suddenly the world of jobs seemed nice, not horrible as I had thought. The manager wanted me to work at his restaurant. He liked me. I should have asked him his name – he knew mine from the application form. Perhaps we could meet after work sometime and go to the cinema together. Maybe I could even ask my mum to cook dinner for him.

I went home at once and told my mum, and obviously she was very pleased. As a treat she made one of my favourite meals, meatballs and spaghetti with tomato sauce. I sang her a song I'd heard about a mouldy old meatball covered in cheese which rolls off the plate, out of the kitchen and lands under a hedge in the garden. I couldn't remember most of the words but she enjoyed it anyway.

After lunch I sat down to watch some of my favourite *Decisions, Decisions* and *Ballroom Blitz* videos, and I made a list of my favourite dresses that you have worn. I managed to narrow down a top 5 for your reference (D.D. stands for *Decisions, Decisions*, B.B. stands for *Ballroom Blitz*):

1) Red lycra (D.D. 13/11/92)
2) Green with double shoulder straps (B.B. 24/6/93)
3) Long black with gloves (D.D. 12/10/92)
4) Mauve with choker (D.D. 19/07/93)
5) Pink with side slit (B.B. 1/6/92)

I hope you agree with my choices. I'll make sure to keep updating the list and fill you in on any changes I make.

I spent the rest of the day in a state of anticipation. My mother ironed my black school trousers and adjusted the waist button so that it would fit. Then she helped me shine my shoes. I put a tiny bit of shoe-shine on the brush labelled Shine On, and scrubbed, with my hand inside the shoe as if it was a puppet. Then I took the Shine Off brush and did the same, but without the shoe-shine.

Then I got my other clothes ready. On the chair in my bedroom I laid out my Global Hypercolour T-shirt and a pair of white towelling socks. I always wear particular T-shirt/sock combinations on each day of the week, except weekends when I wear whatever I feel like. On Monday I wear the Thorpe Park T-shirt my father bought me, along with my white towelling socks with green stripes round the ankle, because Thorpe Park is largely green. On Tuesday, I wear my McDonald's T-shirt, plus my socks with yellow stripes, because that's the colour of the McDonald's magic arch. On Wednesday, it's my Dangermouse T-shirt along with my blue striped socks, for obvious reasons. On Thursdays I wear my Bryan Rogers Dance Tour T-shirt and my red striped socks. On Fridays, as I mentioned above, it's my Global Hypercolour T-shirt, which is my favourite because it's made of special material which changes colour when you sweat.

After that I sat down to write you this letter. I'll make sure to write to you again tomorrow to tell you how I got on.

Yours truly,

Pierre Stone

Dear Marie,

The day began at 9:00 this morning, when my mother came into the my room and opened my curtains. It gave me quite a shock. The experience reminded me of camping with my local scout troop when I was much younger; we were supposed to 'strike camp' at 7:00. I remember I was sleeping next to the patrol leader, because I was new, and he pushed me and told me to wake up, and I said "I am awake" even though I wasn't. Then he told me to get up, and I said "I am up," because I wanted to carry on sleeping. Then he and the rest of the patrol pulled me outside the tent in my sleeping bag. I tried to carry on sleeping, but I couldn't because it was raining.

I stumbled out of bed at about 9:15, and showered using my new collection of Insignia bath products. Insignia's got everything – shampoo and shower gel, deodorant and aftershave – the one all-over smell. Then I got dressed and went downstairs for breakfast. My mother had already made me a cup of tea and it was sitting there on the place-mat, next to a little milk jug, a bowl full of sugar-cubes and a dish for the tea bag. I pulled the tea bag out by its 'tag', allowed the final drops of tea to drip in the mug, and then quickly dropped it into the dish provided. I noticed that there was a little barely visible pool of film on the surface of the tea, which meant that the tea bag had been left to stand for too long. I was going to mention this fact to my mother, but I decided against it.

After I added milk and sugar to my tea, I shook a serving of Frosties into my cereal bowl and asked my mother to pass me the milk from the fridge. I poured the milk over the cereal, and began to eat it, but only from one side of the bowl. Before long I had a pool of milk on one side and a bank of fairly dry Frosties on the other, and was free to alternate between the crunchy cereal and the sugary milk.

When I had finished, my toast was ready: two slices of golden

Mother's Pride. I laid them face down on the plate for several seconds, before turning them over onto their backs. I did this because otherwise the toast is slightly damp. In fact, if you look at the plate while you are turning over your toast, you will notice a toast-shaped patch of moisture which it has given off. I buttered each slice and spread Marmite on one and Lime Marmalade on the other. Then I carefully removed the scraps of fruit rind from the marmalade and put them back in the jar before cutting both slices diagonally in half.

While I ate my toast my mother fussed over me and talked about all the things I had to remember for the day ahead. She was obviously quite excited about the prospect of my new career, but I shut my ears and read Stephanie Beacham's My Kind of Day in *Radio Times* instead. In the article she talks about her beach house, her dolphin friends and her neighbours, who include Jan-Michael Vincent from *Airwolf* and Pierce Brosnan from *Remington Steele*. When I had finished, I wiped my mouth with the kitchen paper provided and went upstairs to clean my teeth.

After that, I got dressed, combed my hair and went downstairs to put on my coat. I had to walk to work, since my last bicycle was crushed under the wheels of a truck. It was about 10:40 and my mother and I both agreed that if I left then, I would get to the restaurant in good time. She seemed happy and I let her give me a kiss, which I wouldn't normally do, but I suppose it was a special occasion. Then I left by the front door and walked all the way down to Shalstone Road, turning left at the end on to Clifford Avenue. At that point I looked at my watch – 10:43. The excitement of getting a job had already worn off so I was beginning to feel apprehensive about going through with it. I slowed my pace as I walked towards the junction with the Foxley Lane, passing Rockinghams Garden Centre.

When I arrived, I stopped at the door and looked through the window. I couldn't see anyone, and my nerves subsided with the thought that I might not have to serve any customers or talk to anyone. I went in as quietly as possible, and stood looking at the chairs stacked upside down on the tables, a sight I had never seen before. Then I heard a voice from the back and a girl with an apron came out towards me. I told her who I was and she introduced herself as Karina. Then she told me to put my coat in the back room and fetch the mop while I was at it, so I could start by cleaning the floor.

As I walked past, I gave her a smile which she returned a little reluctantly. She was tall and thin, with black hair in a ponytail and big black glasses. From her skin colour and her accent I guessed she was an illegal immigrant from some Eastern European country. She probably felt insecure about her job, which was why she was being so rude, but I thought that at this stage it was better not to say anything.

In the back there were sinks, a dishwasher, some lockers and a small table next to a door leading to the kitchen. I went to hang up my coat in an empty locker, and then took the mop and went back in to the restaurant, where Karina was sitting at a table with a big book in front of her. I looked at my mop. It was a big stick with grey stringy bits on the end inside a large bucket covered by a colander. I took the initiative and removed the mop from the bucket, and then I started sweeping the floor with it. After a while I noticed that Karina was looking at me.

"What are you doing?" she said.

"Mopping the floor," I replied.

"But the mop's not wet, Paul. There's no water in the bucket."

"Oh... should there be? I didn't know."

"What do you mean? Haven't you ever used a mop before?"

"Uh... no."

She paused for a moment.

"Well," she said, with an unpleasant edge in her voice, "go back to the sink, put some Flash in the bucket and then fill it up with hot water."

I did as I was told, but I felt a bit angry that she had not explained properly in the first place what she wanted me to do. How was I supposed to do something if she didn't tell me what it was she wanted? She was obviously the sort of person who didn't have time for other people.

When the bucket was full of hot soapy water, I went back and began to mop the floor, starting in the far corner of the room so that Karina couldn't watch what I was doing. I got the hang of it quite quickly. The colander was there so you could squeeze away excess water from the mop head, just like wringing out a flannel before washing your face. And I found it satisfying the way that one could make spiral patterns with the mop on the floor, and then watch as they gradually evaporated, leaving no trace except a cleaner-looking surface. Also, it occurred to me that I could have worked out the importance of water to the mop's function just by thinking about its name – 'mop' rhyming with 'sop', as in 'sopping wet'. A more careful consideration of words and their use could stand one in good stead, I decided.

When I had finished the whole floor I went up to Karina.

"Not bad for a beginner," I said with a grin. "Now what would you like me to do?"

"How about putting the chairs on the floor?" she said, without looking up.

Ignoring her bad manners, I went about the work quickly. I soon discovered that this was a job anyone could do. All it required was a firm grip on the chair with both hands: one hand on the back and the other on the seat. Then one had to employ a simple twisting motion to get it from the table to the floor, right side up. Also, I made sure to arrange the chairs so that they were all facing one another, as if they were having a tea party.

This time when I finished, Karina came up to me. I thought at first she was going to apologize, but then I realized that this was not the case.

"You can clean the tables, now," she said, handing me a bottle of cleaning fluid with a trigger, and a cloth.

I had no objection, but I did wonder what I would have to do to get her to treat me with some respect. Perhaps she was a person who needed to be approached carefully. Anyhow, I got on with the job. The circular wiping motion had a calming influence on me, much like 'Pat' Morita's car-washing exercises had on Ralph Macchio in *The Karate Kid*.

While I cleaned the tables, I couldn't help thinking of you, and imagining you suddenly arriving for lunch helped me clean much better. If you did arrive, there would be no telling which table you'd choose, so I made sure that every one was perfectly clean. No doubt you would pick companions to suit the particular mood in which you found yourself. Perhaps someone like Carol Barnes, the newsreader, who understands your fears and your hopes for the future. Also someone jolly, but caring, like Anneka Rice. Lastly someone with a lot of experience, an internationally known star, like Stefanie Powers from *Hart To Hart*, with her dog, Freeway.

Over lunch you would mention your doubts about your ongoing role in *Decisions, Decisions*. You want to leave to pursue individual projects, but you feel a certain gratitude to Tony for having helped you, and you don't want to abandon him in his old age. Stefanie would say straight away that you shouldn't let anyone come between you and your ambitions, and that you should leave immediately. However, Carol, the voice of reason, would disagree by saying that the future is uncertain, and that leaving could be a decision you'd regret. Anneka would join in by saying that not leaving could be a decision you'd regret, if you end up unhappy and frustrated at having missed your chance.

You listen to all their advice, but lunch isn't the place to talk only about careers, so you move the conversation to talk about nice things like dresses and make-up. After the meal has finished, you say goodbye to everyone and go off alone in your limousine. You ask your chauffeur to drive along the motorway and turn off when you reach some windswept beauty spot. You leave the car and stand there, the air whistling through your hair and chiffon scarf, considering your dilemma. In a way, you enjoy the lack of responsibility you have on *Decisions, Decisions*, because it means you have less to worry about. But deep down you know it's wrong for Tony to be doing everything for you. You want to stay, but at the same time you feel the need to go.

After I had finished cleaning, I put serviettes on every table and then laid out the cutlery: a fork for the left hand and a knife for the right. Then Karina showed me how to lay out the soup spoons. When I had finished that, I took a moment to rest and admire my handiwork. The restaurant looked fit for a star. In fact, it seemed a shame that ordinary people were going to come in and spoil everything.

Then Karina came up to me and told me that soon customers would be arriving. She said she would take care of them, and maybe later I could help. In the meantime, she suggested that I polish the cutlery in the dishwasher. I asked her where I could find the polish, and she said no, just clean them with a tea towel, and then separate them out into knives, forks and spoons.

I went into the back room. The only thing there which could have been a dishwasher was a big metal box next to the sink. I opened it, and immediately got caught in a blast of heat and steam which meant that I had to spend several seconds wiping my glasses with my T-shirt. When the steam finally cleared, I could see that inside the dishwasher was a large plastic tray piled high with cutlery, along with all the other pots and plates. I went to grab hold of it, but it was too hot, so I waited some more until it was sufficiently cool for me to pick up.

I carried the tray over to the sideboard behind the salad bar, so I could watch Karina dealing with customers as I polished and perhaps learn a thing or two. Once I had set the tray down I fetched the plastic cutlery container, which was divided into sections for knives, forks and spoons. Soon I had an efficient system in operation: I would pick up a piece of cutlery in my left hand, and then pass it to my right as if I was giving myself a present. My right hand was covered in a clean tea towel, so the cutlery found itself wrapped in a warm blanket. Then, after giving it a quick rubdown, I would drop it in the box with the rest of its shiny friends. I took care not to touch it with my potentially dirty fingers, holding on to its heel with the towel until the last possible moment, like Achilles' mum dipping him into the river.

"Paul."

It was Karina. "I'm just going down to the wine cellar to get the wine for today. If any customers arrive, just call me and I'll come up, OK?"

"Sure," I said, and carried on polishing.

I watched my hands perform their functions and it was satisfying to see a pile of hot, wet cutlery become a tray full of neat, dry stacks. After several minutes I looked up and, to my surprise, saw two middle-aged women, both rather overdressed, taking off their coats and sitting down at the table next to the window. As I watched, one of them caught my eye and I immediately turned round to look for Karina. Then I remembered where she had gone, and suddenly realized that she had forgotten to tell me where the wine cellar was. Just at that moment, the voice of one of the women came across the room towards me.

"Could we order some drinks?"

I turned to look at her and smiled, a thick smile which seemed to stick to my face. I felt that I should definitely go and fetch Karina, but not only did I have no idea where she was, I was also afraid that the women might think I was ignoring them on purpose and get annoyed. Also I thought that if I did show some initiative, then Karina might treat me with a little more respect. With my heart beating fast, I walked towards the table.

"Hello," I said. "I'm your waiter."

Neither of them said a word. I could tell that they were waiting for me to continue.

"Basically I'm here to ask you what you want to eat, tell the cook, and bring it to you when it's ready. Oh, I forgot, you need menus. You can't just ask for anything you feel like!"

I laughed at this but they didn't seem to find it as funny. After a while I stopped laughing and went to fetch two menus from the rack.

"These are lists of food and drink we have in the restaurant. If it's on the menu, you can order it. If it's not, you can't. If you can't finish your food, don't worry too much, just concentrate on finishing the most expensive thing on the plate. For example, if you were eating hamburger and chips, then you should leave the chips and try to finish the hamburger. There are other things to remember, but I can't think of them all now. What do you want to drink?"

The two women looked at each other for a moment.

"Er... I'll have... a spritzer," said the one on the left.

"I'll have one as well," said the other.

"Two spritzers," I said. "Right. What is a spritzer, exactly?"

"Don't you know? I though you said you were a waiter," said the first one, rudely.

"Yes, I am, but it's my first day," I replied.

"It's white wine and soda water," said the other one, obviously trying to make amends for her friend's rudeness.

"White wine and soda water," I said. "In what sort of glass?"

"In a wine glass, of course,"

"With ice?"

"You can have it with or without."

"Do you want ice?" I said, trying to steer the conversation back to the issue at hand.

"Yes."

"I don't," said the first one.

"Hang on a minute," I said. "Let me just write all this down."

I went to get a pen and paper from the pile I had seen next to the till, and then strode back to the table.

"OK... so that's two glasses of white wine and soda water, one with ice, one without."

On my pad I sketched two pictures of a wine glass filled with a liquid divided in half by a line. I drew bubbles in the top half and wrote 'wine' in the bottom.

"I'll just go and get these drinks, and in the meantime have a look at the menu. Don't worry about dessert, you can order that later."

I left them and went over to the bar area to make the drinks. First I took two wine glasses from the rack above my head, where they were hanging upside down. Next, I looked in the fridge, and saw a bottle of white wine already opened, with a cork sticking out of the top. I removed it and poured a small amount into each glass. Then I put the cork back in the bottle and put the bottle back in the fridge. I peered inside for some soda water, but there was none to be found.

I started to get a little anxious, because from the information I had been given, I could not make one spritzer, let alone two, without soda water. I wished that I had brought my Sodastream with me – I could have made enough soda water just by filling a bottle with ordinary tap water and pressing a button. I thought harder and then I remembered one time I was near a bar with my mother, and I had watched the barman mix her a drink using a strange-looking water-pistol attached to a hose. I looked around and caught sight of the very same thing, attached to a holster in the bar.

I stood up and took hold of the hose-pistol, examining it closely before doing anything. It was made of black plastic, with a silver metal pipe, like you find in a shower, leading from the end of it to a recess below the bar. On its back were two rows of five white buttons – ten in all – numbered with a secret code of letters: C-P-L-T-X/K-Q-F-L-G. These were clearly intended to prevent potential thieves from leaning over the bar when the barman wasn't looking and helping themselves to a dose of their favourite drink. But once again I felt annoyed at Karina, this time for not having told me the meaning of the code. As a result I was as helpless with the machine as the average thief.

Nevertheless, all I needed was some clue as to which letter on which button referred to soda water. I looked up and down both rows, but with no inspiration. I decided that the best way to proceed would be to make exclusions. It was clearly not 'C', as that would be coke, and equally, 'P' was bound to be Pepsi. I also decided that 'L' must mean Lilt, the totally tropical drink, 'T' must mean Tango, and 'X' was probably some poisonous substance which I would be wise not to tamper with.

Looking at the next row, I was stumped immediately by the letter 'K', which did not appear to fit any soft drink that I was familiar with. After a moment's deliberation, I concluded that it most likely referred to an American spelling of Cariba, the once-popular grapefruit and pineapple crush. The next letter, 'Q' seemed more obvious – Quatro, another mixed fruit drink which had enjoyed success after a series of colourful adverts featuring a computerized drinks dispenser.

The letter 'F' struck me as being a reference to Fanta, although since their best-known drink is an orangeade, already represented on the list by Tango, I decided that it was probably another fruit flavour, like apple or lemon. 'L' confused me at first, since it was a repeated letter, but then it occurred to me that it had to be Lucozade, the refreshing glucose drink that used to be advertised on television by Daley Thompson.

'G' was the final letter. For a moment of panic I thought that it couldn't possibly refer to soda water, and that I was not going to be able to complete my mission. But then it hit me – 'G' must be the 'G' in 'G & T', meaning Gin and Tonic, which is made with tonic water, which is almost exactly the same as soda water. This had to be the button which dispensed the all-important liquid. Taking a firm hold of the drinks-pistol, I moved over to the glasses into which I had already poured the wine. I lowered the tip of the gun over the top of the first glass, and, taking careful aim, pressed my thumb down firmly on the 'G' button. To my immense relief, a jet of clear liquid emerged, and as it began to mix with the wine, I saw a flood of bubbles rising to the surface.

After I had topped up both glasses with the soda water, I remembered the ice cubes that the rude lady had requested, and I spooned in a couple from the large white bowl I found on the bar. Then I put them both on a tray and carried it all over to the table, with my fingers spread out underneath, holding it at just over shoulder height.

"Here are your drinks, ladies," I announced. "A spritzer with ice for you... and a spritzer without ice for you."

I laid the glasses down.

"I can see you're still looking at the menu," I said, which I could, because they were both still holding them. "Don't hesitate to call me when you've decided."

I pointed to the salad bar.

"I'll just be over there."

I lowered the tray and walked back towards the bar. Then, unexpectedly, I heard the voice of the second woman.

"Waiter," she said. "Waiter, I'm afraid this drink isn't what we ordered."

"What?" I said, turning round. "What's the matter with it? It's a spritzer, isn't it?"

"Well, it looks like a spritzer, but it tastes... different."

"What do you mean, 'different'?"

"Uh... it tastes too sweet."

"It tastes too sweet?"

"Yes, it tastes too sweet," interrupted the other woman. "In fact, it tastes of lemonade."

I paused for a moment.

"No it doesn't," I said. "You're making it up."

"What? How dare you talk to me like that!"

At that moment I heard the sound of footsteps behind me. I turned to see Karina appearing at my side.

"Is there a problem, Mrs Philips?" she said, glancing at me with a very nasty expression.

"Yes there is! This... man is completely incompetent and when I told him that we had been given the wrong drink, he told me I was lying!"

"I'm terribly sorry about the mistake, Mrs Philips, I'm afraid he's new here. Let me take those, and I'll get the drinks myself – on the house of course. What was it you ordered?"

"Two spritzers."

"Right away."

With that, she took the tray from my hand, placed the glasses on it, and with her other hand grabbed my arm and walked me out and into the back room.

"I think those two are very confused. I think..."

"Shut up!" said Karina, not loudly, but sharply enough to make me stop in my tracks. "I don't care what you think. Not only did you totally ignore my instructions, but you insulted a regular customer and embarrassed this restaurant."

I was speechless. Karina was clearly using this as an opportunity to exert her authority over me in this totally unreasonable way. In the situation, I didn't see any option but to leave before things got any worse. I reached for my coat.

"I'm leaving," I said. "But I'm going to call the manager first thing in the morning and tell him how you've treated me."

"Do whatever you want!" she said, almost laughing.

I put on my coat and turned to leave, but she caught my arm once again. I was beginning to feel aggravated.

"Use the back door, please."

"You won't hear the last of this," I said, as I opened the heavy door and picked my way through the rubbish bags before emerging out on to the street. "I'm going to tell the manager on you."

Outside the light was quite bright, although it was still cold. I looked at my wrist-watch – 12:24. Using my watch's calculator function, I realized that I had been given less than an hour and a half to prove myself in the job. It was ridiculous. Then I looked down and noticed that patches of yellow and orange had emerged on my Global Hypercolour T-shirt. As I walked home through the breeze I watched them gradually disappear. When I got home, my mother wasn't there and she hadn't left a note. After a few minutes of wondering what to do, I decided to write you this letter.

Yours truly,

Pierre Stone

Dear Marie,

This morning I rang up the manager of Portofino, and told him what Karina had done. He sounded sympathetic, but he said that there was nothing he could do about it and he was very busy and had to get off the phone. It's easy to see who wears the trousers in that relationship.

Anyway, this afternoon I decided to go into town to play in the amusement arcade. I do have a computer of my own, a ZX Spectrum, but it broke recently and my mother said that she couldn't afford to get it repaired. My favourite Spectrum games are: Underwürlde, Knight Lore, Manic Miner, Deathchase 2000 and Ant Attack. I also have an Intellivision games console, three Game And Watches and an Etch-a-Sketch.

The arcade I went to is called Game Zone and it's in Croydon. Usually I get there via the number 33 bus, but that stops right outside Portofino, so today I went a bit further to the number 247 bus-stop on Purley Way. On route, I stopped off at Costcutter and bought a Snickers bar. I made a point of referring to it by its real name, Marathon, but the manager didn't seem to notice. After that I got on the bus, and paid for my ticket with the exact change. Luckily the bus wasn't very full so I was able to sit upstairs at the front and pretend to be the driver.

The arcade is just opposite the bus-stop, so when I got off I went straight in, stopping only to look at the window display, which contained Egyptian busts, carriage clocks and other special prizes. At the front of the arcade are two rows of fruit machines, which I walked straight past because they're very boring. At the back are the video games, but before approaching them I went over to the change machine. Change machines are better than fruit machines because you win every time.

I put in a pound and got back two fifties, one of which I put in my right pocket, the other I kept in my hand. Then I headed over towards the video games. The first one in line was

Terminator 2: Judgement Day, a game I've played once before and found quite hard. It involves shooting the heads off an army of robot skeletons. The next game was the one where you are a little Japanese man who has to burst balloons with a corkscrew, but I wasn't in the mood for that.

I quickly surveyed the rest of the games, hoping to see one of my favourites like Gorf, Robotron or Galaxians, but as usual they were nowhere to be found. I used to play those games in Eric Razzle's Razzle Dazzle joke shop near my old house. There was an older boy there called Captain Beaky who taught me how to play all the games, such as the ones I mentioned above plus Defender and Asteroids, although not Pac Man, which he didn't like because he was too good at it and always won. He didn't really teach me, as such. He just looked at the screen and I looked at what he did.

After a moment's reflection, I decided to have a go on Streetfighter II, a kung fu game I had seen before but never actually played. I slipped my fifty pee into the slot; on the screen appeared the words Credits: 2. I chose the Player Two position on the right-hand side, and spread my feet apart to get the best position. I had eight different streetfighters to choose from, mostly men, although there was one girl and also a green monster with orange hair. I browsed through their portraits with my joystick, considering each one in turn. After some thought I decided on Ken, the American with blond hair and red pyjamas, because I didn't want to be anybody foreign.

Then I realized that someone was standing next to me.

"S'aright if I play?" said the stranger.

I looked up. It was a boy, smaller than me and much younger, wearing jeans and an inflatable jacket. Despite his apparent politeness I realized at once that he was intent on invading my space. He should have just watched me play and waited his turn like everybody else, I thought, as I looked around for help.

I didn't want him to play, but I also didn't want to lower myself to his level and be rude. Before I could say a word, he leant forward and punched the Player One button, instantly making it a two-player game and using up my remaining credit. I stood there, paralysed. I couldn't stop him - the damage had already been done. The only thing left was to fight him.

He chose to be a Japanese streetfighter with a pyjama suit much like mine, except in white. On the screen I watched as a plane whisked us off into a fighting arena in Brazil: a patch of earth surrounded by trees and cheering villagers. We faced each other, motionless, and I took a quick glance at my controls. There was a joystick and two rows of three buttons. From the instructions it seemed like the top row was for punches and the bottom for kicks, going from left to right in order of strength - soft, medium and hard.

I didn't have a chance to consider this much longer, however, because I looked up to see him flying towards me, with his foot outstretched. I took a step back but this didn't stop him connecting with my head, causing my neck to snap backwards and my body to fall to the ground. After a moment I gathered my senses and got to my feet, but by the time I was upright my opponent was in the crouching position, and before I could react my legs were cut from under me by a sweeping kick. This time when I regained balance I knew to take a few steps back, but this didn't stop him moving in fast and delivering a series of blows to my face followed by an uppercut which left me standing, shaken, with stars circling around my head.

Helpless, I watched as he moved in again, grabbing hold of my shoulders before turning and throwing me through the air. My flight arced in slow motion and I landed in a crumpled heap. My opponent stood calm in triumph, the wind whistling through his red headscarf.

I felt my face flush and my hands begin to tremble. I knew I had to concentrate to win, using all my video game experience and everything I had learned from Captain Beaky.

Round Two began. I stood still, tensed and expectant and, as before, my opponent came sailing towards me in a flying leap. I waited until the last minute, and just as he was about to connect, I let fly with a maximum strength punch, hitting him mid–air and sending him crashing to the ground. Then I did as he had, and moved into a crouching position, sweeping him to the floor just as he tried to stand up. As soon as he recovered from that I came in with a high kick and then followed up with a punch, which he blocked.

I knew I had to press home my advantage and moved in with a kick and then a punch, both of which he managed to block, and then continued with a jab, which he couldn't. I had him on the ropes and I finished him off with a full strength kick which hit him in three places – head, chest and stomach – and laid him out flat. Knockout! I raised my hand in a fist of triumph, soaking up the shouts of the villagers.

The stage was set for a decisive third round. He knew better than to try his flying kick again, so we both took a few steps back and forth, gauging the situation and waiting for the other to make the first move. I tested a few punches and kicks against the thin air and moved gradually closer. He did the same, and when we were close enough, launched a fist attack which I easily blocked but which allowed me the opportunity to quickly duck and land a strong punch in his mid–section. I followed up with a sweeping kick, but he managed to jump clear of that and then bounce back for an aerial attack on my head which I easily avoided.

I saw my chance and did the unexpected, springing forward to punch, rather than kick him, from the air. Unable to mount a defence, he reeled back and I followed with a searing roundhouse. I knew he was on his last legs and took a moment or two to contemplate the style of my victory.

Just then, I saw my opponent crouch in an unusual position and cross his arms at the wrist. Then, with a cry of "Oh, Eustace!", he launched a ball of blue flame which flew from his outstretched hands towards me and impacted on my chest, knocking me off my feet.

My hands began to tremble with frustration. I struggled upright but before I knew it another blue ball was approaching. I tried leaping out of the way, but in my haste I misjudged the jump and instead landed right in its path. I could only watch in horror as the fireball crashed into me and I fell to the floor, motionless.

I couldn't believe what had happened. Just a second ago I was winning and now I was dead.

"Special move," said my opponent, smiling at me. "Sorry mate."

I quickly started rummaging in my pockets for more money to carry on playing, but before I had found any I turned to see him walking out of the arcade.

I wanted to follow him to demand a rematch, but on checking my change I saw that I only had fifty pee left, which I needed to get home. I decided that I would go home, ask my mum for some more money and then come back and wait for the boy and ask for a rematch, in the meantime practising my special move.

On the bus, I sat down at the back and thought about the fight. I remembered how exciting it was to win that second round, especially the bit when I jabbed him in the face. I examined my hands – my fingers were sore from all the punches I had thrown. Then I thought of the helplessness I felt when he fired those fireballs. I crossed my wrists over as he had, and imagined what it might be like to have that power surging through me.

When I got home my mother was out collecting money door to door for Christian Aid, which I forgot she does every Wednesday. I couldn't find any money in her drawers, so instead I sat down in front of the TV with the peanut butter sandwiches she had left me and a glass of coke from the Sodastream. You probably have a Sodastream in your house – if you don't, you might consider getting one. They're very useful, because you can make everything from orangeade to cherryade to cola. Simply fill a bottle with water, insert it into the special cylinder, and press the button to squirt in the air. After that, add some drops of your favourite flavouring and, hey presto, fizzy drinks.

In bed that night I had another dream which you might like to know about. We were co-presenting *That's Life* – you were Esther Rantzen and I was all three of the male helpers who sit behind the desk. While you were talking to the camera, one of us kept trying to interrupt and add a comment, while another kept hitting him and trying to make him shut up. The other one just sat and watched you talk.

Perhaps the dream meant that you should consider taking over *That's Life*.

Yours truly,

Pierre Stone

Dear Marie,

This morning I had a pleasant surprise, because a brand new video shop has opened a few doors down from the newsagent, where the florist used to be. I knew they were doing something in there, because people have been going in and out for a few weeks, but I didn't know what.

It's quite a small shop, but they have a lot of videos – three walls stacked from floor to ceiling, plus a counter and a chocolate stand. However, I wasn't particularly interested in that, because I'd already bought my chocolate. I won't bother telling you about every video in the shop, but suffice to say there were several different sections, including Comedy, Thriller, Horror and New Releases.

I didn't like the horror section, but the thriller shelf had some interesting things on it, like for example *Steele Justice*, *Remo: Unarmed and Dangerous* and *King Of The Kickboxers*. Also there was *Deadly Prey* starring Troy Donahue and Cameron Mitchell. It's the worst kind of nightmare and for Mike Danton it's come horribly true. One moment he's taking the garbage out – the next he's knocked unconscious, kidnapped and dumped in the depths of a steaming jungle.

The covers in the comedy section had a lot of pictures of young men having fun, in films like *Screwballs*, *Porky's* and *Confessions Of A Window Cleaner*. One film from that section which particularly interested me was *Perfect Timing*. Stephen Markle (*Without a Trace*), Michelle Scarabelli (*Cover Girl*) and Paul Boretski (*Space Hunter*) star in this hilarious comedy about a zany photographer's struggle to keep his job, his girlfriend and his sanity. It's Perfect Timing for a comedy. On the New Releases section my eyes fell on *Lambada Nights*, which seemed just the sort of film that you would like to watch. I took the empty box from the shelf to carry with me as I looked round the rest of the shop.

That got me thinking about what your taste in films might be. I knew that you'd like dancing films, which is why I picked up *Lambada Nights*, so I also took *Footloose*, with Kenny Loggins and Lori Singer, which is one of my favourites. Also, since you're friends with Stefanie Powers, I thought you'd like to see her in her most powerful role yet, starring opposite Ken Kercheval in *All My Sorrows*. It's based on a true story. Also I took *Xanadu*, starring John Travolta and Olivia Newton-John, a tale of aliens and impossible love, plus *The Cannonball Run*, which is my favourite film of all-time.

After looking through all the rest of the films in the shop, I decided to take out all those, as well as *Hercules In New York* starring Arnold Strong. This was actually Arnold Schwarzenegger's first movie but the producers thought they should give him an American-sounding name. I took the boxes over to the counter, which was manned by a bored-looking fat man, probably from Greece. I put the boxes down on the counter.

"Are you a member?" he said.

"No," I replied. "But I'd like to be."

He told me that I needed two forms of identification, one with my address on, to join the club. I didn't realize it was a club, as it looked very much like a shop. I asked the man if I could take the films if I promised to bring them back.

"Sorry, you need to be a member," he said, although I could tell that he wasn't really sorry.

I turned away from the desk, disappointed. Then I realized that I did have some identification with my address on - a letter from my MP, wishing me a happy birthday, which I had kept as a memento. I decided to go home and get it.

When I got home, I saw that my mother's car was outside, which meant that she had got back from shopping. I opened the door and from the hall I could see her unpacking things from boxes in the kitchen. I decided to go upstairs and get those pieces of identification I needed and then go straight out again. However, on the way upstairs I heard an unusual sound from the kitchen. I stopped to listen more carefully.

"Ow!"

It was my mother crying out.

I crept down the stairs. My mother was standing in the middle of the room, between the kitchen table and the sideboard, clutching her head in one hand and a can of Green Giant Niblets in the other.

"OW!" she shouted. Her face was contorted with pain.

I moved closer towards her, interested. The pain seemed to subside and she sort of staggered backwards into a chair.

"F.." she said.

"F?" I said in reply. I couldn't think what it was she was trying to say.

"F.." she continued.

I thought for a moment, looking around at the shopping on the table and the sideboard.

"Fromage frais?" I suggested, holding up a Yoplait four-pack.

"Phone," she said, finally. "Ambulance."

She was having trouble getting the words out and it was obvious that she was having some sort of big problem, so I decided to do what she seemed to be asking. I picked up the phone and dialled 999 as I had been instructed when I was much younger.

The phone rang for a few rings and then a woman's voice answered.

"Police, fire or ambulance," she said. "Which service do you require?"

I paused for a moment before replying: "Ambulance."

There was a 'click' and then I heard a man's voice.

"Ambulance service," he said.

"Yes, could you help, please?" I said, looking at my mother. "I think there's something wrong with my mother's head."

"What's the exact problem?" said the man.

"Ow!" said my mother.

"Well, she keeps shouting, and she has difficulty talking. Also she's holding her head in her hands. She's in pain."

"And you have no idea what caused this."

"That's right," I said. "I just came in and she was like this."

"Is she having difficulty moving?" he asked.

I looked over at my mother. She was slumped against the washing machine.

"Yes," I said.

"Can you give me your address?"

"It's 12 Silverdale Way, Purley, and the postcode is..."

"That's OK," he said, interrupting me. "I don't need the postcode. What's your name?"

"Paul Metcalf," I said.

I should explain that although Pierre Stone is my real name, Paul Metcalf is the name I use in daily life.

"I'll send someone as soon as I can," said the ambulance man, and hung up rather abruptly.

I hung up the phone as well and turned to look at my mother. She hadn't moved, and was still slumped with her hand on her head and her other hand clutching the sweetcorn. I thought it best not to touch her, and tried to make myself useful by unpacking the rest of the shopping while I waited for the ambulance to arrive. I couldn't work out where most of it should go, so I was quite relieved when the doorbell rang.

I opened the door to two ambulance men in uniform, and once they were inside I showed them to the kitchen where my mother was sitting. One of them knelt down next to her and touched her and talked to her, although she didn't seem to respond at all. The other one had a sort of do-it-yourself fold-out wheelchair which he assembled quite quickly and then they both helped to get her into it. Then they wheeled her out of the house, one of them pushing and the other lifting the chair over difficult steps. Before I followed them out of the kitchen, I noticed on the kitchen chair a large wet patch which I decided not to think about.

Outside was the ambulance. They wheeled her to the back of it, and then lowered a metal landing onto the ground and pushed her onto that. Then they raised it, with one of them on board holding on to her. While this was happening I asked the other one if I could come along as well, and he said

60

yes. Luckily I remembered to close the front door before I climbed in.

One of the men drove the ambulance and the other was in the back with me and Mum. He asked me to help him lift her onto a bed, which I did, and once she was lying down he turned her on her side, and then covered her up with a blanket. It was quite amazing to be in an ambulance, driving up the wrong side of the street and straight through traffic lights, although the ambulance men seemed unexcited, I suppose because they do it all the time. We drove in silence, since I couldn't think of anything to say, and instead I looked out the window. I spotted two Dewhurst the butchers along the way, one of which I had never seen before.

After maybe ten minutes we arrived at the hospital, and the ambulance stopped outside an entrance called 'Emergency'. The two ambulance men helped get my mother out of the vehicle in the bed she was in. They wheeled her inside at quite a rate, and I followed, until I was stopped by a nurse in a white uniform who told me that I should wait until the doctors said she was ready for me to see her. The nurse guided me to a seat with a lot of other people. I thought she was going to sit down next to me, but she didn't.

I had a lot to think about – the videos; the video club membership; my mother; the shopping. It occurred to me that I did not know what had happened to the can of Niblets she had been clutching. Presumably, if she still had it, they would remove it and keep it in a safe place.

Then, on the table in front of me, I saw a pile of glossy magazines, including *Bella*, *Take A Break*, *New Woman* and *Homes And Gardens*. All of a sudden I noticed a magazine I had never seen before. It was called *OK!* – Britain's biggest brightest best value celebrity magazine. The front cover announced articles about Telly Savalas, Andie MacDowell and Pamela Anderson from *New Baywatch*, plus Love and Marriage in Crazy Hollywood, and Nigel Havers Cooks His Favourite Lunch.

I turned first to the six page interview with Pamela Anderson.

The 26-year-old star is exposing her talents as CJ Parker in one of the most popular TV shows, *New Baywatch*. "She's one of the best lifeguards on the beach," says Pamela about her on-screen alter ego. "CJ's very spiritual, very earthy, very smart and very athletic." Art imitates life a bit, as Pamela shares CJ's passion for metaphysics, is a voracious reader and has been practising every watersport known to man.

I found the interview very interesting, especially the photographs, which showed Pamela spending some free time painting and simply relaxing in her beautiful home. Elsewhere in the magazine I read about Craig McLachlan, from *Neighbours* and *Grease* fame, who says "my real life is just like a soap". Also there was an interview with Andie MacDowell. She and her husband live a happily married life in this really beautiful house that Paul built with his own hands. "We bought an old log cabin and he redesigned the whole thing. There were no blueprints - he just did it purely by instinct."

No doubt you can understand the pleasant surprise I got on finding this new magazine, especially because you would usually only find old issues of boring things in a doctor's waiting room. This one was brand new and most likely someone had bought it and left it there as a thoughtful gift for someone with a dead or dying parent like myself.

Before long I had read all of the magazine, and as none of the other magazines really appealed to me, I decided that I would go and ask to see my mother.

"I'd like to see my mother," I said to the woman behind the desk.

"Can you give me her name?"

"Mary Metcalf."

"Wait one moment," she said, turning around. "Dr Misra?"

A middle-aged Indian man stepped from a door behind her.

"Dr Misra, Mrs Metcalf's son is here."

He approached me and then put his arm on my shoulder.

"Perhaps we had better sit down," he said, leading me towards a row of chairs.

I sat down and he sat down beside me, looking into my eyes. He had a brown face and glasses.

"I'm going to be perfectly straight with you. Your mother has had a cerebrovascular accident – a stroke. At the moment, she's in a coma."

There was a pause.

"Why?" I asked.

"Well," he replied, "there are three immediate causes of a stroke. Thrombosis, which is basically a blood clot within a brain artery; cerebral embolism, in which another kind of blockage, for example a bubble of air, occurs in an artery; and cerebral haemorrhage, which follows the rupture of a weakened blood vessel in the brain, and is usually the most serious. At the moment we don't know which of these caused your mother's stroke. You probably know that she suffered from hypertension, which is the most likely long-term cause."

"What's a coma?" I asked. I knew what it was but I could sense that he was dying to tell me.

"It's like sleep, but much deeper. It's a state of deep unconsciousness. At the moment we don't know how long it is going to last."

I nodded, looking serious.

"Will she dream at all?"

"Um, no, she is too deeply unconscious for that."

Dr Misra glanced over his shoulder.

"Would you like to see her now?" he said, looking back at me.

"Yes," I replied.

We both got up and went past the woman behind the desk, into a corridor and up to one of the doors on the left-hand side. The doctor opened it and gestured for me to enter first, which I did.

Inside was a small room with a bed, in which lay my mother. It was obvious that she was deeply asleep, as the doctor had said, because her eyes were closed and she wasn't moving. As I got closer I could see that there was a tube inserted into her left arm which led up to a transparent bag on a stand. On the right-hand side of the bed was another tube leading from under the covers to another, yellow plastic bag near the floor.

"What's in those bags?" I asked Dr Misra.

"The transparent bag is a drip, containing glucose solution, which is being injected directly into the bloodstream. It's like a liquid food, because at the moment your mother isn't able to feed herself. The other bag is there to collect her urine, since she isn't able to control her bladder."

"Yes, I know," I said. "Best not to talk about that."

I moved closer towards her, to where her head was lying on the pillow. Her arms were on top of the blanket, partially covered by a nightdress which had a blue printed pattern on it. As I leaned in closer, I could see that it wasn't a pattern, but instead the words Property of Croydon Hospital printed over and over again. Then I looked up at her face and noticed that she had no teeth.

"What's happened to her teeth?" I asked.

"It's practice to remove dentures from stroke victims, in case they accidentally swallow them."

"Dentures? What are they?"

"Dentures – false teeth."

I didn't realize that my mother had false teeth, so this came as quite a surprise. I stood there looking at her for several seconds before Dr Misra spoke again.

"Is there anything else you'd like to know?" he said.

"Do you have any idea when she might wake up?" I said.

"Not at the moment, I'm afraid, Mr Metcalf. We've already run some tests which should tell us more about the exact cause of the injury, so once the results get back we should have more of an idea. Until then, there's very little we can do. Perhaps you'd like to sit with her for a little while?"

"Yes," I replied.

"I'll get the nurse to bring a chair."

He left and within moments a nurse appeared, carrying a plastic chair which she set down beside me. She took a moment to look at my mother and then at me.

"You can talk to her if you want to, love," she said. "There's a good chance she'll be able to understand."

I thanked her and then sat down. She turned and left the room, shutting the door behind her.

I was alone with my mother and for a while I stared at her, looking at her bony fingers and her gums. Her mouth was wide open, and I could hear her breathing. I wanted to reach over and close it, but I knew that you're not supposed to touch sick people.

"Mum," I said. It seemed strange to be talking to someone who looked so asleep, but I didn't want to disappoint the nurse.

"Are you all right?" I said. Then I realized that there was no point in asking questions, since she wasn't able to answer me. I thought I would carry on with just telling her things.

"You're in hospital. I'm here. There's a doctor and a nurse outside. You're in a bed. Er... you're wearing a nightgown. The carpet's purple... sort of purple and blue. There is a table next to the bed, with a lamp on it, and a packet of tissues."

I couldn't think of anything else to say, so I stopped talking. I looked at my mother's hands again. They were very thin, and looked much older than the rest of her, with thick, ropey blue veins winding around the bones. Her nails were very yellow.

There didn't seem much more to do in there, so I decided to go outside and sat down in the same seat as before. There was someone new in the seat beside me, a woman not much older than myself, reading an old copy of *Woman's Own*. She was flicking through it very fast, without paying much attention to what she was reading, so I thought it would be a good opportunity to strike up a conversation.

"I'm waiting for my mother to come out of a coma," I said.

I could tell that I had roused her from some sort of daydream because she looked up sharply.

"Sorry?" she said.

"I was just wondering if you had a friend or relative in a state of deep unconsciousness."

"Er... no. It's my husband... he's got meningitis."

"Meningitis... I've never heard of that."

There was a pause.

"Dr Misra, is it, helping you?"

"No, actually, it's Dr Johnson."

"Oh yes."

Once again, there was a moment of silence, but I felt that it was important for her sake that we continue.

"Helpful, is he?" I asked.

"Yes, he's been very good."

"Yes, so's Dr Misra," I said, leaning towards her. "Very informative."

By the look of her I didn't think that she would have benefited from an explanation of cerebrovascular accidents, so I picked up the copy of *OK!* magazine and had another look at the article on CJ.

After a while I felt myself yawn, and I decided to go in search of something more interesting to do. I put the magazine back on the table, and then walked back and forth in the hall next to the waiting area. After a bit of this I noticed a machine at the end of the corridor, which I recognized as being the sort they have in swimming-baths, which dispense sweets and crisps. I walked towards it at a brisk pace. The front was covered in a glass panel, and on the right was a little black keypad for numbers and a slot for money. The items in the machine were fixed in rows facing forward, wedged in metal coils.

My eyes read the packets from left to right, row by row. The display included roast chicken crisps, prawn cocktail crisps, Breakaway, Fruit Gums and Refreshers. All the items were listed by number (1, 2, 3 etc.), followed by another number indicating the price, for example 23p. I fished in my pocket and took out a good selection of coins. I decided that I was in need of some Refreshers. I inserted twenty pee in the slot and then I tapped in the number corresponding to my choice, which in this case was 12. After only one or two seconds, the metal coil began to uncurl and I watched as a brightly striped tube dropped to the floor below. I leaned down and pushed my hand through the door, which was heavier than it seemed, and grabbed my prize.

I tore open the end, to reveal the top of a stack of pastel-coloured discs. Lifting the first pink one from the top, I examined its concave shape before popping it into my mouth and crushing it with my teeth. Crunchy powder and a sweet, sherbety taste spread over my tongue, and quickly disappeared down my throat.

Then I went to sit back down where I was before. When I got there I noticed that the lady with the sick husband was still in the same seat. She wasn't reading the magazine any more, in fact she wasn't doing anything, so I decided to offer her a sweet.

"Would you like a Refresher?" I said.

Again she looked up with surprise, but I wasn't fazed by this and held the packet up towards her.

"No, thank you," she said, and turned away.

I was surprised but decided not to say anything critical about her behaviour. All the more for me, I thought, and finished off the rest of the packet quite quickly. I shoved a lot of them into my mouth together, crunching them up into a sort of foam and enjoying all the different flavours at the same time.

Then I heard a voice from behind me.

"Mr Metcalf?" It was Dr Misra. I stood up to face him.

"We've just had the results of that MRI scan. Would you like to come into my office?"

I didn't say anything, but I followed him into his office, which was a small room a few doors down from my mother. When we got inside, he gestured for me to sit down in front of his desk, and then he sat behind it.

"I'm afraid the MRI scan didn't give us any good news, Mr Metcalf. It looks as though your mother's stroke was caused by a cerebral haemorrhage."

The doctor removed his glasses.

"That's usually the most serious, isn't it?" I said, removing mine.

"Yes, that's right. It's hard to tell how it will develop; what we do know is that she has suffered near-total paralysis on her left side. It's also unlikely that she will recover consciousness in the immediate future."

There was a pause as I looked at the floor.

"Can I see the MRI scan?" I said, looking up.

"Yes, if you want," said the doctor.

He took an envelope out of his desk and from it produced a black and white sheet of eight little photographs of my mother's brain. Then he went towards the wall and found a transparent box, which he lit up with the flick of a switch. He tucked the sheet of photographs up under the metal clip at the top and I got up to have a closer look. He pointed to one of the photographs.

"If you look close enough you can see damage to this area of the brain, caused by a rupture in the artery supplying this part."

"Oh yes," I said, although I found it quite hard to see, having removed my glasses.

"That's how we know it's a cerebral haemorrhage, not a thrombosis or an embolism."

"Yes."

There was a pause.

"I'm sorry Mr Metcalf."

"It's not your fault!" I said.

Again no one spoke.

"All we can do is wait," said the doctor. "There's really no way to predict what will happen."

"No," I said.

Then the doctor returned to his desk and I followed, resuming my original position in the chair.

"Perhaps you'd like to see her again. Visiting time ends in an hour," said the doctor. "Unless you have any more questions?"

"No, I think I'd prefer to go home," I said, "but I'll come back and see you tomorrow. What time's a good time?"

"Uh... visiting time begins at 10:00."

"In the morning?"

"Yes. 10 to 12 and 2.30 to 8 every day," he said, standing up and putting his glasses back on.

I stood up and put mine back on too, walking with him to the door which he opened for me.

"I'll see you tomorrow," I said. "Thanks for all your help."

I left the reception area and walked towards the exit the way I had come. Outside, I looked for the ambulance I had come in so I could ask for a lift home, but I couldn't find it. It wasn't far from the exit to the number 72 bus–stop, so I went and stood there, waiting, until a bus arrived, and then I got on and bought a ticket from the driver. Then I sat down at the back and he drove me home. There was no one else on the bus whom I could talk to about my mother and her cerebrovascular accident; I considered going to talk to the driver about it, but then I saw the sign which said "Please do not distract the attention of the driver when the bus is moving".

When I got home, I had a glass of milk and watched an hour and a half of Children's BBC. Then I went to find the two pieces of identification I needed for the video club and I went and became a member, although I couldn't take the films out because I forgot that I didn't have any money. I came back empty-handed, and was reminded that my mother was lying in the hospital because I didn't know what I was going to have for dinner. Luckily, at that moment I found a Refresher which was in my pocket, along with all the paper and foil from the packet, and I popped it in my mouth and resolved to suck it for as long as possible. Just then the doorbell rang and I opened the door to the next-door neighbour, Doreen Fox. She had seen Mum being put in the ambulance and she asked me how she was and how I was feeling. I looked at her but I didn't speak, because I wanted to finish sucking the Refresher.

"Yes, don't say anything if you don't want to, dear. You must be in shock. You poor thing. Would you like me to come in and cook you a little dinner?"

"Yes please," I said, swallowing the Refresher. I was hoping she was going to say that.

Before long she had cooked me a meal of Bird's Eye Steakhouse burgers and McCain's Southern Fried chips, together with boiled frozen peas and Heinz Tomato Ketchup. Then she went home after talking to me and holding my hand and saying some prayers for my mum. After that I sat down and wrote you this letter. I hope you've enjoyed it.

Yours truly,

Pierre Stone

Dear Marie,

This morning I emptied out the jar I have of one and two pee pieces and, after counting them, I had £1.64, which is enough to rent one video from the video shop. I went to the shop and had to choose which one to take out of all the ones I had selected the previous day. I couldn't choose *Lambada Nights*, because the boy there said it was a New Release and it cost £2.50. I had to choose between *The Cannonball Run*, *Hooper*, *Xanadu*, *Footloose* and *Hercules In New York*. After some deliberation I chose *The Cannonball Run*. In case you didn't know, it stars Burt Reynolds, Roger Moore and two girls who look like Daisy from *The Dukes of Hazzard*.

I walked home to find Doreen Fox waiting outside the front door. She said that she would give me a lift to the hospital. I had almost forgotten about my arrangement to see Dr Misra, and I quickly put the video through the letter-box for safe keeping before getting into the passenger seat of Doreen Fox's car. Once inside, I remembered Jimmy Saville's advice and Klunk-Klik-ed my seat-belt.

On the way I saw Londis, Spar, Woolworths, Waitrose, Safeways and Rockingham's Garden Centre. We also stopped at two zebra crossings and a pelican crossing. When we arrived, Doreen parked in the car park and we walked into the hospital together, following the signs for Intensive Care. As soon as we arrived there I recognized it from the day before, although there was a different receptionist. Doreen asked the receptionist if it would be all right to go and see Mrs Metcalf, and she in turn asked us to wait. After perhaps a minute Dr Misra appeared.

"I'm afraid I have some bad news for you," he said, looking at us both in turn. "Mrs Metcalf had another very severe stroke. She passed away about an hour ago."

I paused for thought.

"You mean... she's dead."

"Yes."

"Oh I see. I thought you might have meant something else."

"No, I'm afraid not."

"Right."

I glanced at Doreen. She had started to cry; I watched her mouth twitch and her eyes go red. After a while she seemed to calm down, and she dabbed her eyes with a tissue which she kept stuffed in the sleeve of her cardigan.

"Can I see her now?" I said to Dr Misra.

He said that I could. Then I looked over at Doreen. By the look on her face it was obvious that she was feeling a bit left out. With a smile I followed Dr Misra down the corridor.

We turned left and I realized that she must have been moved to a different room, probably so they could keep a closer eye on her, now her condition had deteriorated. As we walked along the corridor, I noticed that the doctor looked slightly uncomfortable and I thought I'd relax him with some friendly chat.

"Do you ever watch Quincy?" I asked.

"Er... I can't say that I do," he replied.

"Well, it's not on any more. It starred Jack Klugman as an expert pathologist. He dealt with cases like this all the time."

"I see... well, pathology isn't exactly my field."

"In that case, if it's ever repeated, I suggest you watch it," I said. "You could probably learn a lot."

After walking quite far, down various staircases, we came to a room labelled Morgue. Dr Misra opened the door and I went in after him. Inside he lead me to a metal table on which was what looked like a body covered in a sheet. We went up to the end of the table, and I watched as he drew back the sheet. Underneath was my mother. She was pale and lay very still, obviously dead.

"You were right," I said. "She's dead."

We both stood and looked at her for a few seconds, and then the doctor asked me if I'd like a little time with her alone.

"No thank you," I said. There didn't seem much point in hanging around.

Once the doctor had replaced the sheet we set off back to the Intensive Care ward where Doreen Fox was still waiting. When we got there, she was sitting down, looking anxious, and smaller than usual. I asked her if we could go home and I turned to shake hands with Dr Misra, thanking him for all his help. He said how sorry he was that it had all been so sudden, and I told him not to worry. Then he left and a nurse appeared with some papers which she said we would need for something called the Death Certificate. I later found out that this was a document designed for the funeral people, so that they could be absolutely sure that the person they were burying/burning was dead.

On the drive home Doreen went on about how sorry she was and how awful it was, etc. When we got home she made me lunch and then we both watched *The Cannonball Run*. Then she talked for a bit about how she would get everything arranged for me with the help of her husband Barry, including making funeral arrangements and getting probate, or something. Then we played Scrabble for a bit and I won quite easily, which surprised me, since I'm not very good at it. After that we played Cluedo and Totopoly, which I also won quite easily. I didn't really want to play but I think she needed something to take her mind off things. Then she made me dinner and after that she left and I wrote you this letter and now I'm off to bed.

Yours truly,

Pierre Stone

Dear Marie,

This afternoon I was bored, so I decided to do something I haven't done for a long time, which is look through the boxes in the attic. I was never allowed up there when I was little, although I always wanted to. The door is a flap in the ceiling, which you pull down using a pole, and then you unfold the ladder, which is in three pieces. Once I had climbed up, I peered inside. It was dark, but I had a torch. As I flashed it around I could see that there were lots of boring old clothes, but also some boxes and chests which did look interesting. I took them down and laid them out on the floor of my mother's bedroom where I could look through them properly.

The first box I looked through contained old packs of playing cards, shoe-horns, letter-openers, and badges, including one which said Desperate Dan's Pie-Eating Club, and another which said I Love My New Gas Cooker. The next one contained a lot of bigger toys, including my old rollerskates (blue suede with yellow plastic flashes down the side), Stretch Armstrong and the Six Million Dollar Man, complete with red tracksuit and plastic trainers. Also in the box was the Bionic Woman, along with her hairbrushes and make-up kit, which I had bought before I realized that it was a girl's toy. Right at the bottom I found an old jar of Green Slime which I thought it best not to open, as well as an advert for Grow Your Own Sea Monkeys which I remembered cutting out from an issue of *Master Of Kung Fu*.

Once I had put that aside, I opened up the biggest box that was in the attic. Inside were my Action Men, including all their clothes and weapons as well as their training tower, their submarine and their multi-terrain vehicle. I carefully removed the men themselves, one by one. They had been stacked in rank, with the most senior at the top and the most junior at the bottom. There are five of them, and together they form the world-famous secret crack commando unit known as

Deathwing. First out was Major John Nelson, who was elected leader partly because he is an old-model Action Man without Eagle Eyes or supergrip hands, and therefore less able to perform in the field. He is dressed in a standard army uniform: black plastic boots, khaki trousers, woollen khaki sweater, scarf and peaked major's hat. Major Nelson is the respected elder statesman of the group, a man of few words who puts the safety of his men above all else.

Next was Captain Steve Weston, second in command and the only blond in the group. Like the rest he is a later model, with a little switch at the back of his head which moves his blue eyes this way and that, and he has rubber fingers. Steve is dressed in a blue uniform most commonly worn for ceremonial occasions, along with black riding boots tucked under his trousers. Steve is seen as something of a go-between, between them and the Major, and is tolerated more than liked. But he is a professional and a good soldier and they respect him for that.

Then came Lieutenant Mike Bronson. Mike is something of a maverick, a man who has served in many different capacities all over the world; perhaps best described as brilliant but unpredictable. He always seems to be there to help the team when they need him, but once the danger has passed he mysteriously disappears. Mike wears his standard adventurer's outfit: safari jacket and trousers with brown plastic knee-length boots, sabre and scabbard, and beige jungle hat. His head is rather bigger than the rest, because in his original box he had been known as 'The Atomic Man', and one of his eyes serves as a microscope, which you can use by looking through a hole in the back of his head.

Next was Sergeant 'G.I.' Joe Baxter, an American marine and the second best sharpshooter in the world. His brown nylon hair is sculpted on his head in such a way as to make him somehow better-looking than the others. Joe wears a scarlet beret, a camouflage jacket, khaki trousers and army boots, and is armed with his ever-present rifle. Generally regarded as the team's secret weapon, he is an extraordinary warrior who can rival anyone in terms of determination and resourcefulness.

Last was Private Bill Johnson, a highly dependable mechanic and weapons expert, who can be relied on to fix any gun or drive any tank. Bill wears olive-green overalls with a machine gun ammunition belt around his chest, army boots and a rubber wool cap. Bill and Joe are best friends and do everything together, including organizing team outings. When they go to a restaurant, the Deathwing members always have the same things: John has liver and bacon, Steve has pizza, Mike orders chicken vindaloo, Joe has a cheeseburger and Bill has fish and chips. They also all have their various likes and dislikes. For example, Bill likes football, whereas Joe likes baseball, and John prefers going to the opera with Steve.

Once I'd had a good look at all the Action Men, I put them back into their container and went on to the last box, which was a small wooden chest. I opened the catch and inside I saw that there were only a few items: a black and white photograph of a couple in the street, one of whom was a younger version of my mother, the other I guessed to be my father. Underneath that there was a box with a medal inside it. Right at the bottom there was a fairly large pistol, together with a small blue cardboard box. I picked up the pistol – it was heavier than it looked, and had a long barrel. With a bit of effort I managed to yank out the revolving section, and saw that all the spaces for bullets were empty. As you might have guessed, the blue box was full of bullets, and I put six into the spaces provided, just for safe keeping. Then I put everything back in the chest and took all the boxes back up the stairs and into the attic, but not before trying on my rollerskates and skating round on the living room carpet for a few minutes.

Yours truly,

Pierre Stone

Dear Marie,

Today was the day of my mother's funeral. Doreen and Barry Fox picked me up at 2:45 from my house to get to the chapel by 3:15, which is when the service was meant to start. It's only down the road, so we got there a little early, about 3:00, and once Barry had parked the car we walked around the cemetery for a few minutes. I was wearing my best clothes, as Doreen had suggested: my blazer, brown check trousers, navy blue shirt and striped yellow tie. Also I was wearing my socks with pigs and clouds on them. The shirt was only short sleeved, but since I was wearing a jacket that didn't matter.

Then we went to the chapel, and while we were waiting outside I took a couple of photos of Doreen and Barry with my camera. As I was doing that a woman approached us. I didn't recognize her, but I could tell that Doreen did. She introduced herself as Miriam Moule, from Christian Aid. She was a bit nervous and she talked quite fast about what a great help my mother had been, and how kind she was, and how helpful she had been, etc.

I couldn't think of anything to say but luckily the vicar soon appeared. He seemed friendly and nice, although I didn't like his hair, which was scraped over the top of his head to hide the fact that he was bald. I took a photograph of him and then he shook all our hands and guided us into the chapel. It was much bigger than I had expected, with quite a lot of pews and a pulpit for the vicar in the right-hand corner. In the middle, where the altar normally would be, was a sort of table made of rollers leading back towards some curtains in the wall. Beside the table on both sides were big vases of flowers, so I took some photos of those too.

We settled down in a pew, second from the front on the right-hand side, just in front of the pulpit. The vicar was nowhere to be seen, and nothing happened for several minutes.

I looked over at Miriam and saw that she was kneeling on a cushion, with her hands clasped on the hymn-rail in front of her, eyes closed. I looked at Barry, and then he looked back at me. Next the vicar appeared and went up into the pulpit.

Barry handed me a little booklet; I watched him open his and then turned to the same page myself.

"Please stand," said the vicar, and we all did, although it took Miriam a bit longer. "Jesus said, 'I am the resurrection, and I am the life; he who believes in me, though he die, yet shall he live, and whoever lives and believes in me shall never die.'"

I thought about this for a moment but I couldn't understand it. I was going to ask the vicar to repeat himself but then I remembered what Mr Mellett told us in primary school – in church you're not supposed to clap or ask questions.

"The eternal God is your refuge and underneath are the everlasting arms."

This seemed to make more sense, and after considering it for a few moments I noticed that the vicar was standing quite still, looking to the back of the church. Soon everyone turned their heads to look back with him. We saw two men coming through the door, carrying a box on their shoulders. One of them had a beard and they were walking in a strange way, as if going up stairs one step at a time. The box was quite small and seemed quite light, and it came as a surprise when I realized it was the coffin that contained my mother. The men walked all the way to the roller-table, and set the box down on it before turning and leaving through a door on the left.

Then the vicar said the words, "Heavenly Father" quite loudly and everyone joined in with this prayer:

"Heavenly Father,
In your son Jesus Christ
You have given us a true faith and a sure hope.
Strengthen this faith and hope in us all our days,
That we may live as those who believe in
the communion of saints,
the forgiveness of sins,

and the resurrection to eternal life;
Through your son Jesus Christ our Lord.
Amen."

I quite liked the prayer, but I was getting pretty tired of standing up and I was disappointed when the vicar said to read Psalm 23. I read it along with everyone else – it was about sheep lying down in green pastures and walking through the valley of the shadow of death – but I wasn't paying that much attention.

After that we finally got to sit down, although I had to stand up again briefly to let Doreen Fox get past. She walked over to the lectern on the other side of the room, and then opened the book which she had brought with her.

"The reading is taken from the Gospel of John, Chapter 14, Verses 1 to 6," she said, looking up at us for a moment. "Jesus said to his disciples, 'Do not let your hearts be troubled. Trust in God still, and trust in me. There are many rooms in my father's house; if there were not, I should have told you. I am going now to prepare a place for you, and after I have gone and prepared you a place, I shall return to take you with me; so that where I am you may be too. You know the way to the place where I am going.' Thomas said, 'Lord, we do not know where you are going, so how can we know the way?' Jesus said, 'I am the way, the truth and the life. No one can come to the father except through me.'"

This speech made me think about a lot of things.

After the reading Doreen Fox came down and sat back in the pew, and then the vicar, who had been sitting listening, stood up in his pulpit.

"Dear friends," he said, I suppose addressing us, although he was looking somewhere down the middle of the chapel, so it was hard to tell.

"We are gathered here today to mourn the passing of our beloved Susan, who was so cruelly taken away from us."

For a moment I thought I might be in the wrong funeral. Then I realized that he didn't know my mother was called by her second name, Mary. It made me want to laugh, but I didn't.

"Susan leaves behind a son, Paul, many friends and happy memories. In her kindness she spent many years working for charity, particularly with her local branch of Christian Aid. She married Charles Metcalf in 1962 and became a mother in 1965, a role which continued despite the death of her husband. We remember her generosity, her many talents, and her love for her family and friends."

I saw the vicar put away the piece of paper he was reading from, and then he said: "Now please join me in singing hymn number 141 in your hymn books."

We stood up to sing the hymn, and at the end the vicar said, "Let us pray," and we all kneeled.

"Lord have mercy upon us," said the vicar.

"Christ have mercy upon us," we replied.

"Lord have mercy upon us," he said.

Then we all said the Lord's Prayer and after that the vicar read another prayer.

"Let us commend our sister Susan to the mercy of God our maker and redeemer," he said. "Heavenly Father, by your mighty power you gave us life, and in your love you have given us new love in Christ Jesus. We entrust Susan to your merciful keeping: in the faith of Jesus Christ your son, our Lord, who died and rose again to save us, and is now alive and reigns with you and the Holy Spirit in glory for ever."

"Amen," I said, along with Doreen, Barry, and Miriam.

"We have entrusted our sister Susan to God's merciful keeping and we now commit her body to be cremated: earth to earth, ashes to ashes, dust to dust: in sure and certain hope of the resurrection to eternal life through our Lord Jesus Christ, who died, was buried, and rose again for us. To him be glory for ever and ever."

At that moment, as if by magic, the coffin began to move backwards on the table towards the curtain, slowly, until finally it went through and disappeared completely. I strained up to see what the vicar was doing with his hands but I couldn't see any buttons or switches.

Then the organ began to play and the vicar left the pulpit. We were all still kneeling and we kept kneeling for what seemed like years, until Barry stood up, and I stood up, and then everyone else did. Then we walked down the aisle and out of the chapel in a line, with me first. The vicar was by the door and as I approached he reached out and we shook hands.

"About the lesson that Doreen read," I said. "How are you supposed to get to the father's house?"

"Well... in the lesson, Jesus said that none can come to the father except through him."

"But what does that mean?"

"It means that only if you believe in Christ can you come to the father."

"I believe in Christ. But how do I get into the father's house? And where is it? And how many rooms does it have?"

"Perhaps you should come to church if you want to find out more," he said. "I preach at St. Mark's in Kenley every Sunday. We'd be more than happy to see you there."

He seemed eager to end the conversation. I looked round and saw everyone standing behind me and I realized that I was blocking their way, so I moved on and went out of the chapel. Then I waited outside for everyone else to shake hands and exchange words with the vicar, and I took a photograph of each person as they came out. Before long, Miriam left and I got in the car with Doreen and Barry and we drove home. When we got home, Doreen invited me in for tea but I said I was feeling tired so I could go home and write all this down for you.

Thank you for reading this.

Yours truly,

Pierre Stone

Dear Marie,

Today I woke up quite late, at about 11:00, with a start, because I'd had a nightmare. I dreamt that my mother and I were on a traffic island in the middle of some futuristic spaghetti junction, and I was on a bicycle and my mother kept trying to make me go out into the road with all these huge juggernauts and lorries. Eventually I did, and it was very scary. I didn't get very far before I woke up.

When I got up, I put my dressing gown on, and then I went downstairs to get my breakfast. I had some Coco Pops, but unfortunately I finished the milk so there wasn't anything left for my tea. Then I noticed the puddle of milk at the bottom of my bowl and realized I could use that. The tea tasted very nice, quite sweet and a little bit chocolatey. After that I switched on the radio and tuned in to Melody FM. It's London's easiest and brightest radio station, and they played some good songs, like 'The Tracks Of My Tears' by Colin Blunstone.

While I thought of what to do with the day, I heard a noise at the door and I went up to see some envelopes lying on the doormat. I opened the first one, and found a card with a picture of a vase of flowers on the front, and "In Deepest Sympathy" in gold letters on the front. Inside was a message that read:

> *"The most caring thoughts*
> *are with you today,*
> *expressing the sympathy*
> *words cannot say."*

At the bottom it said, "Please don't hesitate to call round if you need anything. With love from Doreen and Barry Fox." The next envelope contained the latest issue of *Innovations* – tomorrow's products today. These included: a miniature alternative to binoculars; a foldaway rain suit; neoprene fitness shorts; the sonic molechaser; a multi–purpose expanding bag; volcanic rock deodorizer; shogun knives; a bed on a shelf; pet vac and the barkbuster.

In the third envelope was a letter from Ian Rennie telling me about Rennie Decorating Services, which he has been running since 1984. He enclosed his phone number, but I decided to call him later, because Doreen Fox's card made me remember the money. Last week Doreen put all the money that was in my mother's bank into my building society – £10,234. That plus the £12.75 that was already in there made a total of £10,246 and 75p. I decided that today would be a perfect opportunity to go out and spend it.

I ran up the stairs to get dressed. I put on my stone washed jeans, with my Capital Radio T-shirt and my white jacket from Avanti at C&A. On my feet I wore my white trainers with the velcro straps. Then I combed my hair, took my Abbey National Share Account book from my desk drawer and went out of the house.

I walked past Costcutter and the video shop, down the street and over the railway bridge and carried on until I got to the High Street. The High Street is one of my favourite streets because it is full of shops. My first stop was the building society, and when I got there I went straight in and joined the queue for the cashier. I was behind an old lady and a fat man wearing a shirt. While I waited and the queue moved gradually closer, I had a look at a few leaflets about Tessa, Regular Saver and Action Saver, and before long it was my turn. I went up to the window and there was a girl sitting behind it. She had dark hair a little bit like yours but shorter, big brown eyes and a nice smile. I could see by her badge that her name was Karen.

"I'd like to take out some money from my account," I said, placing the booklet into the gap in the see-through wall between us. She reached out and picked it up, sliding off its plastic cover.

"If you'd just like to fill in this form, sir," said Karen, passing me a slip of printed paper.

I looked at it for a little while.

"Just fill in the amount you want to withdraw, and then put your signature."

I picked up a pen which was fixed by a chain to a black blob, and moved a bit closer to it, since it wouldn't come closer to me. I looked up at the girl, but she couldn't see me, she was tapping things into the computer. I hovered the tip over the box marked Amount. Then I let the pen touch the paper, and I saw myself draw a straight line followed by two circles.

I signed it and passed the form back through the wall. My hand was shaking a bit but I was sure Karen didn't notice. She took the form and then ran my account book through a little machine next to her computer.

"How would you like the money?" she said, without looking up.

"In notes."

She looked up at me. "I mean in what denomination?"

"Er..."

"Which notes?"

"Oh, I see... um... OK then. One fifty, one twenty, one ten, and two fives. What's that?"

She paused. "Ninety."

"All right. Another five, and five pound coins – no, nine pound coins – and one fifty, and a twenty – and a ten – and two fives – and three twos – and three ones. And two halves."

"Hang on – I'm sorry. You'll have to start again. And I'm afraid halves are no longer legal currency."

"OK – nine pound coins; one fifty; one twenty; a ten; two fives; three twos, and four ones," I said, slowly.

She finished counting out the coins from a little drawer next to her, and then took the notes she had already counted, and counted them out in my direction.

"Fifty, seventy, eighty, eighty five, ninety... and ten pounds in change," she said, placing the money in the gap in the window, along with my account book.

"Thanks very much," I said, putting the book and the money into my pocket.

I gave Karen a winning smile, and then left the building society and went out into the street. I walked up to the zebra crossing and saw that the red man was standing, so I stood and waited.

I pushed the button on the box fixed to the traffic light, and watched the message flash up on the screen:

WAIT.

I did so, and stood still for several seconds, watching the cars go past. After a while, when there seemed no sign that the man was going to turn green, I pressed the button again, but still with no success. I carried on waiting, getting annoyed. It occurred to me, not for the first time, that the box was there just to give pedestrians something to do while waiting. It seemed stupid to design a machine which did nothing but tell you to do something that you were already doing very well by yourself, and I punched the button again, hard, to make the point.

Before long the lights did change, and I walked quickly across and approached the entrance to Superdrug. As I went towards the doors, they opened by themselves and I walked through them like a character from *Space: 1999*.

The first thing I noticed in the shop was a rack of magazines, most of which were old ones I had seen before. However, one thing caught my eye – *TV Quick*, which had Kimberley Davies (Annelise) from *Neighbours* on the front cover and inside a survey of The Ten Most Beautiful Women On TV. I picked it up and looked inside. They were Gaby Roslin, Kimberley Davies, Dani Behr, Anna Friel, Catherine Zeta Jones, Pamela Anderson, Tania Bryer, Ulrika Jonsson, Natalie Imbruglia, and Patsy Kensit, who is never on TV. I read the article again but I still couldn't see your name or picture anywhere, which was confusing. Perhaps the list was for the ten most beautiful women on TV after you.

I put the magazine down and picked up a basket before starting to walk through the shop. On the left hand side, I noticed a selection of travel goods, including the First Class Travel Wet Pouch. This travel wet pouch:

– is waterproof when swimming

- keeps all items dry and safe
- is fashionable and easy to wear
- one size fits all.

I also saw the First Class Slumber Shades, which aid restful sleep while travelling. You'll find both these items enclosed. I thought you might find them useful on your next trip abroad, be it business or pleasure. If you wanted to swim in your hotel pool and sleep shortly after, then you could put your Slumber Shades in your Travel Wet Pouch, and once you had finished swimming, settle down on a lilo, remove your Slumber Shades and put them on to aid restful sleep.

Further on up the aisle I saw a selection of deodorant and anti-perspirant products. I thought of which might appeal to you, and started to compare the merits of Superdrug Biarritz body spray versus Superdrug Rio body spray. The former has a delicate long lasting fragrance that leaves you feeling refreshed and feminine all day long, whereas the latter contains a subtle fragrance which will linger all day, leaving you feeling fresh and feminine. After a few minutes reflection, I still couldn't decide which one to buy. I did manage to pick up some Mum body responsive 24 hour anti-perspirant protection for myself.

Further along the shelf I came across the range of Impulse body spray which I thought might interest you. Impulse body spray is a gentle deodorant and a high quality fragrance. Use it all over your body, anytime, and you'll feel refreshed, revitalised and confident. I spent several minutes examining the shelf, trying to decide which fragrance would best suit you, but the choice was just too great. I've listed the fragrances on offer below and I'd be grateful if you wrote to me saying which one you would prefer:

- Night Rhythms
- Flamenco
- Avant Garde
- Temptation
- Musk
- Free Spirit

- Captivation
- Impressions
- Vive
- Nirvana
- Chic
- Jeunesse
- Fresco
- Dynamique.

There was nothing else on that shelf which interested me, so I went round to the next aisle. The first thing on display there was the range of Natural Selection products. There was Exfoliating Body Scrub with Sea Holly and Algin; Body Firming Bath Soak with Sea Kelp and Ivy; Body Conditioning After Bath Lotion with Sea Moss and Vitamin E, and Invigorating Shower Gel with Samphire and Seaweed. I didn't buy any of those things, although I enjoyed reading about them.

Before I went up to the counter to pay, I picked up a couple of other items, like Diplodocus foam bath, fish and frog fun soap, Insignia Olympian shower gel (because my supply of Insignia Original has expired), and a packet of Man-size tissues. Luckily there was no queue at the counter, so I went up with my basket to pay. When the assistant came to the Mum deodorant, she didn't comment on it.

"That's not actually for my mum," I said. "She died of a stroke. That's why I've got all this money."

The woman stopped what she was doing and looked up.

"That's... I'm sorry," she said.

"Don't worry, it's not your problem," I said.

After that she finished counting up all my things and told me how much they all cost. I can't remember how much it was, but it was much less than I had in my pocket and I paid with one of the notes.

After packing everything I had bought into a plastic bag, I went out and carried on walking down the street. Before long I came across Waitrose the supermarket, and decided to take a trolley and go in to see what I could find.

The first thing I came across was the alcohol section, full of things like wine and beer and vodka and gin. This was really none of my business, so I went past and headed straight for the area marked Cakes.

When I got there, I was struck immediately by the wide range of cakes on offer, including a selection of Mr Kipling's slices to be enjoyed by all the family. These include: Lemon Slices; Almond Slices; Country Slices; Rich Chocolate Slices; Caramel Shortcakes; Strawberry Shortcakes; Bramley Apple Shortcakes; Bakewell Slices; Cherry Slices and Chocolate Fudge Slices. They all looked nice and after some thought I realized that I could easily afford all of them and put one of each in my trolley.

Then I went to the top of the aisle and turned left, passing by a disgusting cabinet full of dead fish which I thought was very unsuitable to be left in the middle of a supermarket. After collecting a Kellogg's Variety Pack from the breakfast cereal shelf, I visited the canned goods section, which seemed very well suited to a bachelor on his own like me. I picked up some Heinz Baked Beans with Pork Sausages, and Heinz Dinosaur Spaghetti Shapes with Mini Meat Boulders.

At that point I stopped in my tracks, unsure of where to go next. Then out of the corner of my eye I noticed Karen, the girl I had met at the Abbey National, striding purposefully along with a shopping basket in her hand. I was surprised that she had been allowed out of the building society during office hours, but she looked very much at home and I thought it would be a good idea to see which products she was choosing.

First she went to the dairy shelf, and selected some Philadelphia cream cheese and a tub of Delight low-fat spread. I followed quietly behind her and put the same two items in my trolley. Next she went to the fruit and vegetable section, and we both picked out a bunch of bananas and some mushrooms in a punnet. After that we got some canned tuna fish, a jar of pesto sauce, some Uncle Ben's rice and a stick of French bread from the bread department. Then I followed her down to the checkouts, driving my trolley quite slowly so as not to disturb her with my squeaky wheels.

I was thinking of joining the back of her queue when I looked up and saw the sign above it saying "Eight Items Or Less". I knew I had more than eight items, and I didn't want to cause a scene, so I reversed my trolley and swerved into the next checkout. The person in front of me had left a little notice saying "Next Customer Please" on the conveyor belt, and I began to place all my things right behind it. When I had finished, I built a low wall with my boxes of Mr Kipling's cakes, so the person behind me wouldn't know what I was having for dinner.

After I had paid for everything and put the food back in the trolley, Karen was nowhere to be seen, so I just wheeled it out of the shop and into the street. I was too tired to do any more shopping that day, and I wanted to get home so I could send you your presents.

When I got home I parked the trolley behind a hedge, went in and sat down to have lunch. I didn't have time to cook anything, so instead I just picked out things that were ready to eat. First I tore open the Honey Nut Loops from the Kellogg's Variety Pack, tipped the loops into my mouth, crunched them up and swallowed them. They were quite nice and sweet but a bit wheatier than I expected. After I had finished, my mouth felt quite dry, so I washed them down with some old coke I had left in the fridge.

Then I thought I'd try something more savoury, so I used the tin opener to open the can of Heinz Dinosaur Spaghetti Shapes with Mini Meat Boulders, and got out a fork from the drawer. Inside, it was just like the label had promised, with pasta dinosaurs bobbing next to mini boulders of meat. I prodded them for a while before digging in and getting a mouthful of dinosaur, boulder and prehistoric tomato sauce. It didn't take me long to finish the whole can, although I did manage to spill some on my T-shirt.

After that I thought it was time for some pudding, so I tore open Mr Kipling's Strawberry Shortcakes, which I finished in record time. Once I had finished all that I felt a bit ill, and I went up the stairs to have a lie down. On the way up, I passed the dirty clothes basket, took off my T-shirt and put it in. Then I had a little nap and then I wrote this.

Yours truly,

Pierre Stone

Dear Marie,

This morning for breakfast I had a bowl of Ricicles, but I couldn't be bothered to buy any milk from Costcutter so I had them with water instead. After breakfast I watched *This Morning*, and also some of *Good Morning With Ann And Nick* during the advert breaks. On *Good Morning With Ann And Nick*, Nicholas Parsons presented a picture of Tania Bryer with a beard drawn on and you had to guess who it was.

After that I decided to take my ZX Spectrum to Dixons in Croydon to get it fixed. As you may remember, I told you that it was broken. I went to the shower and cleaned myself as usual, and then changed into my grey trousers from Top Man along with my father's old cardigan and my Dunlop Brown Flash trainers. Then I put my computer into a plastic bag and left the house. I walked over the bridge towards the main road, looking at the people in the street and playing with the rubber buttons on the Spectrum.

When I got to the building society, I went in and saw that there was no queue, just one man at Karen's window. The other window was free but I wanted to wait for the man to finish. Quite soon he left, and I went up and presented my booklet. Then I noticed that it wasn't Karen behind the desk.

"Where's Karen?" I said to the woman who was sitting in her chair. She was much older than Karen, more my mother's age. From her badge I could tell that her name was Maureen.

"Karen's not here today," she said.

"Why?" I asked.

"It's her day off," she said. "Do you want to leave her a message?"

"No," I said, fingering my booklet. "Just let me have some money, please."

I passed the book through the gap in the glass. I would have liked to have seen Karen, but I wanted the money. I could always come back later to see her.

Maureen passed me a slip just as Karen had done the day before, although without her grace. I filled in the form, this time a one with three noughts, and then passed it back.

"How would you like the money?" said Maureen.

"Just in twenties," I said. I didn't want to waste time on all that.

When I got the money and the book back, I went straight out of the shop, and then turned towards the bus-stop, to wait for the bus to Croydon. There are more shops in Croydon. The bus soon arrived and I got on, paid my 70 pee fare with the exact change, and sat down just behind the driver, so I would be able to get off the bus as quickly as possible. As we drove, I fingered the notes inside the booklet and then put the whole lot inside my zip-up right-hand pocket for safe keeping.

When the bus stopped, I got off using the double doors. The first shop I saw was Our Price, and I went straight in. Inside were a lot of records and tapes and compact discs. The first album I saw was Take That - *Everything Changes*, which I had wanted to get for a long time and I picked that up immediately, along with the new 7" single from Bad Boys Inc. After that I went over to the Easy Listening section. I couldn't find anything by Colin Blunstone, The Rippingtons or Russ Peterson, but I did find *Lovescape* by Neil Diamond, and *Hey!* by Julio Iglesias. I also picked up *Completely Hooked* by Dr Hook and *The Magic Of Nana Mouskouri*, as well as *More Stars of Las Vegas* and *Music From The 1993 Royal Tournament*.

I went up to the counter to pay for those and the man behind the counter took the records and typed their prices into his till. Then I gave him the money. He didn't say anything, but I suppose there wasn't that much to say.

Once out of the shop, I thought about where to go next. Looking down, I noticed my Dunlop Brown Flash shoes and it occurred to me that it would be a good idea to update my footwear. I knew that there was a sports shoe shop round the corner, and I set off in that direction. Once inside I went straight up to the boy behind the counter.

"I'm looking for a new pair of trainers," I said. "Do you have

Dunlop Green Flashes in size 11?"

"Er... Dunlop Green Flash?"

"Orange Flash would do."

"Er... I'm sorry, we don't stock either of those. I'm not even sure they're made any more."

I hadn't expected this.

"Why don't you have a look at our newer stock, see if there's anything you like," he said, helpfully, and pointed to a rack of trainers on the wall behind me. I rested my bags on the floor and went up to look at them.

All the shoes were on their own little shelf with name tags explaining who made them and how. After a bit of browsing I came across one that caught my attention. It had leather straps going across the top and a lot of complex designs which I couldn't begin to describe properly. Reading the label, I discovered that it was a Reebok Trek Off Road HXL. It's a versatile off-road trainer with sculpted Eva midsole with hexalite heelpad for superior shock attenuation and a highly abrasion resistant carbon rubber outsole, uppers are heavyweight nylon mesh with medial and lateral synthetic overstays. Built on a supportive semi-straight last.

I thought this sounded interesting, so I asked the boy who was working there to get me a pair in size 11. While he went to fetch them, I had a look in the section labelled Ladies Trainers to see if there was a pair that you might like, to help you with your jogging and exercise regime. One which caught my eye was the Nike Women's Air Pegasus IX. This ladies' semi-curve lasted running shoe is extremely versatile: a BRS1000–rubber waffle outsole provides multi-surface traction whilst a rearfoot air unit in a phylon/P.U. interlocked midsole provides excellent cushioning. A Duromesh upper with a synthetic suede/leather trim provides support and comfort.

I sat down on the little settee in the middle of the shop, and took off my Brown Flashes. I looked at my white towelling socks and hoped that my feet didn't smell, because I haven't had a bath since my mother died.

Then the boy came out of the room at the back of the shop with a pair of Reebok Trek Off Road HXLs. He took the shoes out of the box and handed them to me to try on. They seemed to fit very well, although it took me a while to do the laces properly and tie up all the straps. I stood up and walked around the shop while he watched. The hexalite heelpad made walking very comfortable, and after six or seven circuits of the shop I told the boy that I wanted to buy them. I took them off and he put them back in the box.

After I paid for them, I said "Thank you" and left. Outside I stood for a moment and wondered where to go next, before I remembered that I needed to get my computer mended, and I crossed the road towards Dixons.

The entrance was a passageway with glass cabinets on either side. Inside the cabinets were watches, cameras, camcorders, radios, and tape recorders. I looked at them for a while, and then walked into the shop itself. At the back was a wall of television sets which were showing *Neighbours*. I went and watched for a bit. When the scene changed, I changed which set I was looking at, just for fun.

Then a man came up to talk to me.

"Can I help you, sir?" he said. He was short and wearing a suit and big round glasses.

"Yes please. My ZX Spectrum is broken and I'd like to get it fixed," I said, handing him the bag.

"I'm afraid we don't stock those computers any more," he said, not taking the bag.

I let it hang down again at my side.

"So you can't mend it," I said.

"I'm afraid not."

I hadn't expected this either. I stood there for a moment, thinking, gripping the bag a little tighter.

"We do stock many other computers. Perhaps you'd like to have a look at some?" said the man.

"Do they have games?" I asked.

"Yes, we have a complete range of games for the Sega Mega

Drive and Snes game consoles."

"Can I have a look at them?"

"Certainly sir," said the man, and led me over to a rack of colourful plastic boxes. There were a lot of games to choose from. One of the games that caught my eye was Mystic Defender. Azuchi Castle – huge, terrifying, and out of reach. It's where the beautiful Alexandra is held prisoner, facing a deadly ordeal. You are Yamato, incredible warrior and possessor of Magic. Can you reach the maniac genius Zareth before he steals Alexandra's soul!

I looked at the rest of the games, like Dick Tracy, Jungle Strike and Dragon's Fury, and they all looked good. I took Dragon's Fury and Mystic Defender over to the man in the suit, who was fiddling with a rack of blank tapes.

"I'd like both those games," I said. "And a lot of others, but I don't have a games console."

He looked at one of the boxes in my hand. "This one's for the Sega Mega Drive." Then he looked at me. "Would you like to buy a Mega Drive?"

I was surprised. I didn't know what to say. Then I thought more about what he had said and about all the money I had in my pocket. I could feel my heart begin to beat faster.

"Yes..." I heard myself say. "I think so."

Then he took me over to a shelf piled with big boxes. He pointed to one with a picture of a black plastic machine on the front.

"The Mega Drive retails for £99.99. It comes inclusive with a free game, Sonic the Hedgehog."

£99.99... I thought of the money I had got from Maureen this morning, and the money I had already spent on records and trainers. I definitely could afford to buy it.

"I'll have it," I said suddenly.

"OK," said the man, picking the box from the shelf. "Is there anything else you'd like?"

"Yes," I said, squeezing the game boxes in my hand. "A Snes. And the games."

"Which games, sir?"

"A... all of them."

The man didn't say anything for a second. Then he said 'Certainly, sir', and led me over to the counter, put my box on top of it and asked me to wait there while he got everything together. After some minutes he had filled up a couple of big Dixons bags and started to add it all up on the till. The bags on the counter were so full that I could hardly see over the top of them.

Eventually he told me the total price and I handed over the money. Then he gave me my change, along with the receipt.

"Thank you," I said, and walked briskly out of the shop.

Holding the bags tightly in either hand, I stood outside and tried to think of what to do next. I decided to get on the next bus home, so I could try out my new games as quickly as possible. When the bus came, I got on, paid my fare, collected my change and then put my bags down in the area reserved for prams and shopping.

I sat down and as the bus moved off I glanced occasionally at the bags in front of me to check that no one was stealing them. Then, out of the corner of my eye, I noticed a pair of hairy forearms cross the back of my seat.

"Are those bags heavy?" said a voice. I quickly worked out that the person behind me was leaning forward and talking into my ear. I didn't say anything – instead I looked out of the window.

"I bet they are," he said. Now he was leaning further forward. His voice sounded threatening, like one of those villains in *Minder* or *The Professionals*.

"Go on – hit me with one."

I didn't know what to do. I certainly didn't want to do what he was suggesting.

"Go on," he said, leaning over some more. "Just hit me once. Right here."

I glanced over and saw that he was touching his chin.

"Come on, just once. Just hit me one time. Just once. Just pick up the bag and do it."

By this stage he was almost pleading with me. I was getting a bit nervous, but then I noticed that the bus was coming into a bus-stop. It wasn't the stop I wanted, but I decided that it would be better to get off now than stay on the bus with this strange man.

"I'm sorry," I said, picking up the bags in front of me. "I'd like to, but I can't. Thanks for asking."

With that I left my seat and stepped off the bus just as the doors were closing. I walked home as fast as I could, and on the way I thought about what had happened. I decided that the man had probably done a crime and wanted to be punished for it. When I got home I put my luggage down on the sofa in the front room, went into the kitchen and helped myself to a box of Mr Kipling's Chocolate Fudge Slices.

Then I went back and sat on the floor and opened the box containing the Sega Mega Drive. I read the instructions, and plugged it into the wall with one lead, and into the back of the television with another. After I had found the right channel on my TV, I got the Sonic the Hedgehog game out of the bag and opened the box.

I put in the cartridge and flicked the switch. The word SEGA appeared on the screen, and a voice sang it softly and slowly. Then I took out the instruction manual and turned to the chapter called 'Playing the Game'. MURSKAA TOHTORI ROBOTNIK! Tohtori Ivo Robotnik, hullu tiedemies, sieppaa viattomia eläimia ja muutaa ne ilkeiksi robooteiksi! I read this a couple of times before I realized that it was one of seven other languages that the makers had thoughtfully included in the manual for the benefit of foreign people.

Finding the English version, I read on: CRUSH DR ROBOTNIK! Dr Ivo Robotnik, the mad scientist, is snatching innocent animals and turning them into evil robots! Help Sonic fight hordes of metal maniacs and do the loop with the Super Sonic Spin Attack.

The game started in Zone 1, Green Hill Zone. I ran to and fro across green hills, jumping over waterfalls and rolling through underground tunnels. I had to avoid flying fish and bees and stop myself from falling onto pointy metal spikes. At the end, I had to jump from ledges onto the head of a floating professor whom I guessed was Dr Robotnik. He looked a lot like Wilf Lunn, the real life TV scientist. After that was Marble Zone, which involved more running and jumping and avoiding spikes. It was harder than Green Hill Zone and I kept dying. Eventually a message on the screen came up saying Game Over. I was quite shocked that a computer which I had paid all that money for told me that I had to stop playing when I wanted to continue, and I stood up and went into the kitchen to have some Caramel Shortcakes. Then I had some Bramley Apple Shortcakes and some Bakewell Slices, and decided to go back to the computer to carry on playing. I got quite far on Mystic Defender, although I didn't rescue the princess. Final Zone was much harder and I didn't really know how to play, despite reading the instructions a few times. After that I decided to stop playing and I went upstairs to write this letter to you.

Yours truly,

Pierre Stone

Dear Marie,

How are you? Sorry I haven't written for so long. I've been busy playing a lot of Sega and Snes and I haven't really had time to think about anything else. This week has given me the chance to try out all the different games. I've decided that my favourite is Micro Machines, where you get in a car and race around various household objects.

Did you get my letter dated 10th of October? I was wondering if you had received the Slumber Shades and Travel Wet Pouch. Also, you may remember that I offered to buy you your choice of fragrance(s) from the Impulse range. In case that letter didn't get to you, or you mislaid it, the fragrances on offer are: Night Rhythms; Flamenco; Avant Garde; Temptation, Musk; Free Spirit; Captivation; Impressions; Vive; Nirvana; Chic; Jeunesse; Fresco and Dynamique.

Things are OK here, although I sometimes wish my mother was still around, because it's hard to manage a whole house by yourself. I wonder if you have the same problems with your house that I do. Sometimes it becomes very cold here and at other times much too hot. Also, all the bins are very full, and one of the light bulbs in my room has gone black and doesn't work, which makes it hard to read in bed.

I finished all the food I'd bought, so yesterday for lunch I had some jelly cubes and some Oxo cubes and pretended I was an astronaut. Today I went back to Waitrose but everything was exactly the same as it was before so it didn't take long to get bored.

Yours truly,

Pierre Stone

PS: Try looking through the crack in the door of the fridge when you close it and see what happens.

Dear Marie,

This afternoon I was feeling tired, so I went to have a lie down on my mother's bed. It felt strange lying on my mother's bed, because it is a double bed and has two pillows, and my head was resting between them. It's much bigger than my bed and in fact her room is bigger all round. I have been thinking that perhaps I should make her room my room, and my room could become the spare room, where guests such as yourself could stay if they came round.

There are lots of wardrobes in her room and a dressing-up table. After a while of lying there I decided to go and sit at the dressing-up table. On the table there are brushes and powder puffs, as you might expect, but also other things such as pencils. Probably she used her dressing-up table as a letter-writing desk. I wonder who she wrote to. I suppose we'll never know.

There is also a treasure box containing some rings. I had a look at them and then tried them on. There were lots of rings in there so I had one for each finger. When I finished, my hands looked like the hands of the Mandarin, arch-enemy of Iron Man, the famous Marvel comics superhero (I used to read comics when I was less mature than I am now).

The Mandarin is a Chinese villain, probably a cousin or at least a friend of Fu Manchu. He has ten powerful rings on his fingers, all of which do something special. For example: ice; lasers; a bomb; psychic crystal; grappling hooks; force-field and invisibility. I can't remember them all, suffice to say that Iron Man finds him a tricky opponent.

Even though the Mandarin has a ring on his wedding finger, I don't know if the Mandarin is married, would like to be, or doesn't believe in the wedding finger. Perhaps that ring contains a hypno-ray with which he plans to win a bride.

I kept wearing the rings as I looked around my mother's room. In the wardrobes, you won't be surprised to hear, were a lot of clothes. They looked like clothes you might find in a charity shop. There were also shoes but I don't think a charity shop would sell shoes.

Then I had a look through the chest of drawers by her bedside. There was newspaper lining the bottom of all the drawers, which I took out and had a look at. All the stories were very old but some were quite interesting, for example a story about the changing fortunes of the rouble.

Then I looked through what was in the drawers. It was mainly underwear, for example: pants. She had lots of different styles of pants. Some big, some not so big, some white, some other colours. In the bottom drawer I found something which wasn't anything like pants. It was white and plastic and looked like a rocket ship. I was surprised that my mother would still have toys like this when I myself had given them up long ago.

I examined the toy and used my hands to move it through the air as if it was a rocket. At the base of the toy was a wheel you can turn. I turned it and the toy started to hum and vibrate. I suppose this is as good a way as any of imitating a rocket slicing through the atmosphere.

Holding the toy with my ringed fingers, I then imagined that I was the Mandarin and that this was my special weapon, like a light sabre but even more deadly. Perhaps a 'sound sabre' which uses a high frequency sound to hurtle back any opponent, even Iron Man. I found that by turning the base of the sound sabre, I could increase the frequency of the sound, thereby creating a wall of force and decimating an army of masked robots.

It seemed like a very good game. I wondered what my mother had imagined it being – probably just an ordinary rocket. I felt sure that the sound sabre was a lot more fun. Not to say that she is less imaginative than me, only that she had probably read on the original packet that it was a rocket and left it at that.

After a while I became bored of the sound sabre and lay back down on the bed, this time diagonally so that my head rested on a pillow. I wondered if my mother had had any men to spend the night in her bed since my father died that I hadn't noticed. It was possible. I decided not to think about it. It's none of my business and anyway, if she had done such a thing, she would be paying the price in heaven.

Yours truly,

Pierre Stone

PS: As usual, you will find my address on the back of the envelope.

Dear Ms Carpenter,

My name is Pierre Stone and, although we've never met, we have a mutual friend in Marie Mitchell, presenter of *Decisions, Decisions* and *Ballroom Blitz*. I am writing to you out of concern for Ms Mitchell's mental condition.

Ms Mitchell has become uncommunicative of late and I am worried that this is linked to some inner crisis or difficulty which she is reluctant to talk about. As I'm sure you're aware, she has been under a lot of pressure recently, trying to decide whether to move on from *Decisions, Decisions*. She may be experiencing anxiety related to this, resulting in her inability to write a simple letter.

Having experienced a similar problem, I thought you might have an extra-special understanding of what she is, quote-unquote, going through, and be able to lend her a feminine ear. You may feel a certain amount of bitter rivalry over the fact that she took your job, but I would ask you to put it aside for the time being.

I would be grateful if you could keep this correspondence confidential, as I wouldn't want Ms Mitchell to think that you and I have entered into a special relationship which in some way threatens the relationship she has with me.

Thank you very much for your attention in this matter.

Yours truly,

Pierre Stone

Dear Marie,

You probably think I have no experience of women and know nothing about them, but this isn't true.

When I was 16 I met a girl called Tracey on the railway bridge. I used to go there occasionally to watch the trains speed past and other trains speed past the other way. On this particular day, I was approached by a girl crossing the bridge whom I later learned was called Tracey. She asked me what I was doing and I told her. We watched the trains together for a time. When I said I was going back to my house, she asked if she could come and I said yes.

My mother was not in and we sat on the sofa in the living room and listened to the soundtrack from *Grease*. I remember the song 'Learn To Hand Jive' by Johnny Casino And The Gamblers was playing and she started doing a hand-jive. I tried to follow but I couldn't keep up. It seemed funny and we laughed. After the record finished, I switched on the radio and we listened to the Radio 1 chart rundown. During the chart rundown she kept looking up at me, but not saying anything. I don't understand why, but if she had asked me a question, I would have answered it.

After that I heard the key turn in the lock. We both jumped. Not literally, but you know what I mean. We didn't have a chance to talk before my mother came in. She was very surprised to see Tracey there but she wasn't angry. In fact, she was friendly and invited Tracey to have sausages. After that the fun seemed to disappear. I don't think Tracey wanted to have the sausages but she was too polite to say. We stayed in the living room and listened to the rest of the rundown in silence, apart from the music and sizzling.

In the kitchen, my mother watched us eat our sausages, then Tracey went home. I waited for her on the bridge everyday for the next two weeks, but she didn't turn up. Then one day she did turn up but she was with a friend. She looked straight at me but didn't even say hello.

I wrote her a few letters and folded them up and stuck them in the cracks in the bridge. I went back to check on them every day and they were gone, but I don't know if she read them. Once I found one opened on the floor of the bridge with a shoe-mark on it, but I don't think it was her shoe-mark. It looked more like a boot-mark than a shoe-mark.

I saw her again three and a half years later at a bus-stop. She was on her own. I was on my own too, but I didn't bother trying to have a conversation. I thought that if she had wanted to have a conversation with me she would have looked at me that day on the bridge. I looked at her face for a long time but she didn't notice, she was lost in a dream, about what I don't know. Her face looked older and she was wearing a lot of make-up. Her clothes made her look like a prostitute but apart from that she was fine.

When the bus arrived she got on it but I didn't, even though it was my bus. There was no one else left at the bus-stop, so I decided to sit in the seat she'd been sitting in. The seat felt warm and I imagined what had been sitting on it. Then I started to feel sick so I stood up and walked to the next bus-stop. I never saw her again.

Yours truly,

Pierre Stone

PS: I'm not as stupid as I look. I worked out that the thing in my mother's drawer wasn't a so-called rocket after all.

Dear Marie,

This afternoon I woke up feeling a bit sweaty and uncomfortable, because I had fallen asleep on the settee after playing computers all night. I was still wearing all my clothes when I got up, so I went upstairs, took them off and put them in the dirty clothes basket. I decided not to bother having a shower, so I just wiped myself with a towel and put on some clean clothes. Then after that I went downstairs and had a can of Heinz Baked Beans with Sausages.

After that I sat down to think of what to do. I felt like a bit of fresh air and maybe a change of activity, so I decided to go down to the Midland Pub and have a game on the pinball machine, which I had played once before when looking for a job.

I reserved a pocket at the front of my trousers for coins, so that it would be quicker to find them and put them into the machine. I left the house and set off down the road, and it wasn't long before I arrived in front of the double doors of the pub. I pushed them open and went inside. It was a little more crowded than before – there were a couple of men playing pool in the corner and a woman at the bar, but I walked quickly straight up to the pinball table.

When I got there I had a big surprise. It wasn't the same one as before, with the lady robot – it was a completely new game, called Getaway. On the painting at the back was a red sports car racing away from lots of policemen. The table itself was all motorways and flyovers and white dotted lines, like real roads. It didn't look at all like the sort of game I would like, but I had come all that way, so I put a 50 pee piece in anyway and had one go. It was loud and very difficult to play, with lots of flashing red police lights and things which shot my ball back too fast.

I didn't do very well and the game was over quite quickly. I didn't feel like playing again and for a moment I couldn't think of what to do. I still had some money in my pocket and I didn't want to go home quite yet, so I decided to go over to the bar, and ask for a Coca-Cola with ice. I had never ordered a drink from a pub before, so I was a little bit unsure, but I figured that it would be just like any other shop. The barmaid wasn't serving anyone, she was just talking to the woman at the bar, so I didn't have to wait long before she came over to me.

"I'd like a Coca-Cola, please, with ice."

She nodded, and went over to get a glass.

"Thirsty work?" said a voice to my left.

I turned round and saw the woman who had been talking to the barmaid, sitting at the bar with a glass in front of her. She was quite old with long curly black hair and tight jeans with a copper-coloured zip at the ankle. She was also wearing a shiny white shirt. I had never met her before, but it was obvious that she was talking to me. I looked away and watched the barmaid fill my glass with ice.

"Thirsty work, is it, playing that?" she said again.

"Yes, I suppose so," I said, not looking up.

"Did you 'Getaway', then, did you?" she said, and started to laugh.

I looked up. I could see that her eyes were half closed and that her whole face looked a bit sloppy. She didn't look like my mother looked when she was drinking, but I could tell that she was drunk. Then the barmaid gave me my Coca-Cola, and I paid for it with a pound.

"Just ignore her," said the barmaid. "She got fired from her job today."

I got my change, picked up my drink and headed for the door.

"Oi, where are you going?" she said, loudly. "You can't 'Getaway' from me that easily!"

She started to laugh again, and I stopped in my tracks. I realized that I couldn't just walk out of the pub, because I was still holding the glass containing my Coca-Cola. I couldn't just go on ignoring her, so I turned slowly round.

"Sorry," I said. "I didn't mean to get away from you exactly, I just..."

"Oh, don't listen to me, love, I'm pissed as a fart!" she said, and started laughing again. I was a bit shocked by her language and I stood there, clutching my drink and unsure of what to do. Then she stopped laughing and I noticed her expression change.

"Don't worry, sweetheart, I won't bite," she said, softly.

After a moment's hesitation, I moved back towards the bar and sat down carefully on a stool which was next to hers, except for a support beam which came between us. She took another sip from her glass. Even when she wasn't talking her face moved – her lip quivered or her cheek twitched.

"It's my birthday today," she said.

"Happy birthday," I replied.

"Guess how old I am. Go on, guess."

I looked at her as she looked at me. I didn't really want to guess, but I didn't want to offend her.

"21?" I said.

"21?" She burst out laughing. "Oi, Deb, did you hear that? 21, he says I am! 21! That's a laugh. You're a silver-tongued devil, you are."

I didn't know what to say to this so I just sipped my drink.

"What are you drinking, then?" she said.

"Coca-Cola."

"Coke? Just coke? We can't be having that, not on my birthday. Deb?" she said, calling for the barmaid. "Deb, get a shot of Bacardi in that right now!"

"No thanks," I said suddenly, holding my hand over my glass.

"Wha's that? No?" she said, turning to face me. "Don't you want to celebrate my birthday?"

"I do, but..." She was looking at me expectantly now. "But I don't drink."

"You don't drink? Why not? Don't you like it?"

"No... I don't know. I've never had a drink. Well, I mean I've drunk drinks before, but never alcohol."

"What, not once? Never?" Her mouth was open and she looked very surprised.

"No. Never."

"How old are you, love?"

"28."

"28 and you've never had a drink before. Well I'll be." She paused for thought. "Don't you wanna have a go?"

"No, thank you," I said. "I'm not really supposed to."

"What? Who says?"

"My..." I was going to say 'My mother', but then I remembered that she wasn't alive any more. "No one."

"Well there you are then! C'mon, les' have a drink. Deb! Bacardi and coke for... my friend here. Wha's your name?"

"Paul."

"Bacardi and coke for Paul. Make it a double! On the double!" she said, and started to laugh again.

I hadn't even finished my coke yet, but I watched as the barmaid filled another glass with ice and then held it underneath a large upside down bottle of Bacardi Rum fixed to the wall. She pressed it up to the nozzle and liquid began to pour down. After a few seconds it stopped and I saw bubbles swim upwards to the top/bottom of the bottle. Then she brought the glass over to the bar and squirted coke into it from the drinks pistol, and when she had filled it up, she handed it to me.

"Go on then, drink up!" said the woman beside me.

I reached out and took hold of the glass. It was cold.

"Cheers!" she said, holding up her glass.

I lifted mine cautiously and she reached out and clinked hers against it, before lifting her glass to her mouth and taking a swig. My glass remained where it was, in mid-air.

"Go on," she said. "Do yourself a favour!"

I kept hold of the glass. It looked a lot like coke, I thought, so it wouldn't taste too bad. Out of the corner of my eye I could see the woman smiling and trying to encourage me. I lifted the glass closer to my mouth. Why not have a go, I thought. I pressed the glass against my bottom lip and tipped it up, until the liquid came into my mouth and quickly slipped down my throat. It didn't taste too bad, quite sweet, and I was relieved when I finally put the glass back down on the bar.

"There you go! That's more like it!" said the woman next to me.

"Th – thank you," I said.

She laughed again, but this time it was more of a chuckle. "By the way, my name's Jan."

She put her hand out and I took it.

"Pleased to meet you," I said.

She smiled. "You're an odd one, ain't ya? A bit of a gentleman."

I didn't know quite what she meant, but I smiled back anyway. My insides were feeling warm after having a sip of my drink, and I sat in silence for a few moments, trying to collect my thoughts.

"Lemme guess... you're a Virgo, right?"

I looked up, shocked.

"Yes... I am. How did you know?"

She chuckled again. "I knew it. I'm a Scorpio, me. Sting in my tail," she said, and took another swig from her glass.

"What're you doin' here, anyway? Haven't you got a job to go to?" she said, looking up, her head shaking a little bit.

"No," I replied. "I did have a job as a waiter, but I... stopped that. Now I just live at home by myself, since my mother died."

"Oh," she said, frowning. "I'm sorry 'bout that. That's a shame. Getting on, was she, your mum?"

"Er... I think she was about 45. She didn't ever talk about her age."

"My mum was 64 when she popped it."

We sat in silence for a little while longer and I took another sip of my drink. I was quite enjoying it. It made my head feel warm.

"Lost my job today... can you believe that? Three years at a place and they give you the boot just like that... Fucking unbelievable."

I think I must have gone red when she said this, because she burst out laughing again.

"Pardon my French," she said, when she had stopped laughing.

Then she finished her drink, and asked the barmaid for another one.

"I'll pay for that, if you want," I said, remembering the money I had in my pocket and thinking about the fact that she had bought me mine.

"That's very kind of you. You're a real gentleman. Last of the gentlemen," she said to herself and laughed.

The barmaid brought her another drink and while she drank hers I had some more of mine. I was feeling quite hot, despite the ice in my drink, and I took off my coat and put it on the stool beside me.

Then Jan turned towards me, looking me in the eye and holding her gaze.

"Paul," she said. "Would you say I was attractive?"

I felt my face flush, and I turned away and quickly had a gulp of my drink. I felt hot and uncomfortable. I wasn't used to being talked to in this way.

"Go on," she said. "I know I'm old enough to be your mum, but I've still got it, haven't I?"

I stayed where I was, looking at the bar. Then I felt her hand on my leg. I turned round to see her face right next to mine and I could smell the gin on her breath. She was wearing purple lipstick and her teeth were a bit yellow.

"Do you find me attractive?" she said, in a whisper.

I swallowed but I didn't turn my head away.

"Y – yes," I said.

She smiled and took her hand away from me. Then she turned back to the bar and took another sip of her drink. I looked around to see if Deb had heard our conversation, but she was nowhere to be seen.

"You're a nice lad, Paul," she said, without looking up.

"You're nice, too," I said, without thinking.

She turned to look at me.

"Nah, you're just saying that. You wouldn't want to go with an old tart like me."

She moved a bit closer towards me, putting her feet on my stool.

"I'd eat you for breakfast."

I looked at her mouth and her teeth.

"Yes."

She stayed in the same position, while picking up her drink and taking a sip. I did the same. I was looking straight into her big brown eyes and I watched her purple lips move as she swept her hair off her shoulders.

"So... you gonna take me back to your place?"

"If you want."

"It depends what you want."

She put her hand on my leg.

"I... want."

She squeezed my leg and smiled. Then she looked over my shoulder and I followed her gaze to see a man, older than me and with coffee-coloured skin and very short hair, walking over to us. She took her hand and her feet away from me as he approached.

"Steve," she said.

"Alright Jan," he replied, and then he looked at me. "Who's this then?"

"This is my new friend Paul," she said.

"Hello," I said.

"'Allo mate," he said, and then paused as he looked at me. "Do you fancy my wife, then? She's hot stuff, in't she."

I didn't know what to say, or do. I looked at Jan but she just laughed.

"Don't be mean, Steve, he's a good kid."

Steve carried on staring at me. He was wearing a long brown leather coat and he looked quite scary.

"You're all right, mate," he said, although I wasn't sure he meant it. Then he reached out and put his hand round the back of my neck and squeezed. He didn't squeeze very hard, though, and it didn't last very long. Then he turned to speak to Jan.

"I've got to get the stuff out of the van round the corner, you know, for tonight."

"All right, I'll see you in a minute," she replied, and then he went back out of the door.

When he had gone I turned to Jan.

"Was he really your husband?" I said, weakly.

She laughed. "No, no - he's just a mate. He was having you

on, love."

"Oh – right." I was relieved to hear this.

"He's playing in a band here tonight," she said. "That's what he's going to get – you know, the equipment."

"Oh."

"Listen, love," she said, coming closer towards me and whispering. "I've just got to go and give him a hand bringing some stuff in, and then I'll come back and we'll go back to your place. OK loverboy?"

"OK," I said.

She kept on looking into my eyes but she didn't say anything, and neither did I. Then she leant in a little closer, and touched my cheeks with her hands. Her face became bigger as she came nearer, and I felt her lips touch mine. I could feel what must have been her tongue touch my teeth and then slip inside my mouth. I opened it a little and her tongue went right inside. At the same time she squeezed my face with her hands. Then after moving it about for a bit she took out her tongue.

"Th – thanks," I said, wiping my mouth.

"Don't you go away now."

She got up, a little unsteadily, straightening her shirt. I watched her walk towards the door, slowly, staggering a bit. When she had gone I turned round to face the bar, picked up my drink and quickly finished it off. My face was flushed, my skin felt hot and strange, and I had to lean against the bar for several seconds.

When I lifted up my head, my eyelids felt heavy and I was a bit dizzy. I picked up my jacket from the stool beside me and put it on, which proved a bit more difficult than I had expected. Then I looked at my watch – 5:49. I hoped Jan would be back soon. I waited there for quite a long time – as I waited, I watched Deb come back to the bar and wash glasses and do various jobs which I had done in Portofino. I looked at my watch again – 6:02. She had been gone for almost fifteen minutes, and I was beginning to get worried – what if something had happened to her? I decided to go out and see if I could find her.

I stood up from the stool, and then found myself leaning

against the pillar next to me. My legs felt funny, but I managed to prop myself up and then walk slowly towards the door, supporting myself on chairs and tables. It was a bit like wearing rollerskates for the first time. When I was outside the door, I looked to my left down Brighton Road, but I couldn't see anyone or any van that might be Steve's. On my right was the turning for Foxley Lane, and I remembered that Steve had said that the van was 'round the corner'. I decided that it must be there, and I turned to walk slowly in that direction. Before long I turned the corner, but there was no van in sight. I couldn't understand it. Then I thought: Steve must have put Jan in the back of the van and kidnapped her. I turned round and went back into the pub.

"Excuse me," I said to Deb, the barmaid, as I approached the bar. "You've got to call the police. Jan's been kidnapped by that man."

She heard me talking and turned round to look at me.

"What?" she said. "What are you talking about?"

"Jan," I said. "You've got to call the police. She's been kidnapped by that man."

"Which man? What are you talking about?"

"I'm talking about the man who just came in here," I said, getting annoyed now. She obviously didn't understand the severity of the situation.

"What did he look like?" she replied.

"He was black, you know, with short hair. He said his name was Steve."

When she heard this she immediately started laughing.

"You daft sod," she said. "Steve's her husband. He's not going to go and kidnap her, now is he?"

I was surprised by this and it took me a moment to say anything.

"But when he said she was his wife, she said that he was having me on," I said.

"Don't be daft," she said. "She was the one having you on, if she said that."

I put my hand to my mouth and didn't say a word. I felt a bit unwell. My stomach was starting to feel quite ill and I turned away from the bar and started to walk towards the Gentlemen's Toilets. I could feel my insides churning and I was feeling sick. I started to worry that I was going to throw up, and I walked faster. I could feel things trying to rise inside me, so I started to run. I knew I was about to be sick, and I covered my mouth with my hand. Then I felt my stomach spasm. Half-digested food shot up my throat and into my mouth, and some of it flew out through the gaps in my fingers and sprayed against the door as I pushed it open.

When I got into the toilet, I saw that there was a man over by the urinal, and I raised my hand to say something like 'excuse me' while I was running over to the basin with my other hand over my mouth, and bits dripping down. I managed to control myself till I got to the basin, and then I threw up into that. At first I was making quite loud noises and the sick was quite solid, but then it became all runny and clear, and it started to burn the back of my throat. After I had thrown up a few times, I started to cough and retch and very little came, only bits and pieces which I spat into the sink. Then my stomach seemed to calm down, and after I had spat out the last few things, I cupped my hand under the cold tap, turned it on and had a few sips of water. I swilled the first round my mouth and spat like you do when you clean your teeth, and then I gargled the next one and swallowed.

I noticed that the man by the urinal had gone by this point, and I went over to the hand towel and wiped my mouth. The basin was still full of all my sick. I went over and looked at it. It smelt disgusting, and I knew I had to do something about it. I held my nose and plunged my hand down into it, trying to find the plug, but it wasn't there. I realized that the drain must be blocked. The cuff of my shirt was now a bit dirty, but I wiped most of that off with the hand towel.

I decided to try cupping my hands together, scooping up as much sick as possible and then going over to the lavatory and decanting it into the bowl. I repeated this a couple of times, but a lot of it dripped out of my hand and onto the floor. I changed my mind and rolled up my sleeve, dipping my hand into the basin until my fingers were at the plughole. Then I started to dig up the solid matter that was there and push it to one side, letting the liquid drain away.

Unfortunately, the plughole blocked up very soon after I unblocked it, so I had to keep doing it over and over again and very little sick went down each time. I was there for quite a while, and during that time a couple of men walked in and used the urinal. Luckily, they didn't want to use the basin, so I didn't have to explain exactly what I was doing.

Once all the sick had drained away, I got a wodge of toilet paper from the lavatory and wiped up what was left in the basin, throwing the paper into the toilet when I had finished. I did this a few times, and then I turned on the taps and washed what was left down the plughole, cleaning my hands at the same time. Then I took another wodge of paper and wiped the extra sick off the door and the floor and the walls. Then I wiped what was left off my shirt and trousers, and walked quickly out of the pub without looking at anyone. Once outside I walked all the way home, and then I had another drink of water and sat down and wrote you this.

Yours faithfully,

Pierre Stone

Dear Marie,

It seems to me that women are different from men. Not in the way that they are devious and deceitful, because men can be like that too, but in other ways, like the way men can be seen working and doing things around the house while the women complain.

Also women have quite different bodies. I don't want to go into detail but you know what I mean. Perhaps women are made nervous by this and it accounts for their strange, some would say horrible behaviour. I would appreciate your thoughts on this matter, although no doubt you will have your own opinions and be biased.

I haven't been back to the pub in case I saw that woman again. Also, there's no need to go back because the new pinball machine is rubbish. Probably Deb behind the bar chose the new one but clearly she doesn't know anything about pinball, which is hardly surprising, although it should be surprising, considering she's in charge of the pinball.

Yours "faithfully",

Pierre Stone

Dear Marie,

I've been thinking a lot about Pamela Anderson, the actress who plays CJ Parker in *Baywatch*. What do you think about her? I think it would be difficult for anyone to say that she wasn't attractive. She has a lovely voice and nice lips. Plus when she's playing the role of CJ she clearly has a great time, not to mention powerful thighs.

Perhaps you don't like her because you're jealous of the success she is having. *Baywatch* is one of the most popular programmes in the history of television and Pamela Anderson is seen and loved by millions across the globe. This is not to say that *Decisions, Decisions* and *Ballroom Blitz* are not any good, only that they're not nearly as popular or successful.

Also, another thing about Pamela Anderson is that a lot of men would say she is the most beautiful woman they have ever seen. They admire everything about her. I don't think you should find this threatening. In fact, it would be a good opportunity to think generously about another person who is more successful than you. Here are a few facts you could think about that would help you to do this:

Pamela Anderson's face.
Pamela Anderson's body.
How much money Pamela Anderson earns.
How many people like Pamela Anderson.

No doubt you will be as successful as Pamela Anderson one day, if you work hard and behave in a friendly and considerate manner to your fans and people who write to you.

Yours truly,

Pierre Stone

Dear Marie,

Hello. I thought I'd just write to tell you about what I've been doing lately.

Do you remember that girl I met at the Abbey National? Her name is Karen. Yesterday morning I went back there in my new trainers and went up to her window. I passed my book through the gap as usual, and she counted out the money and handed it to me. Just as I was about to leave, she spoke.

"You always come here, take money out and then just leave," she said.

I was surprised.

"What do you mean?"

"Don't you find me attractive?" she said as she ran her fingers through her hair.

"Um... I suppose so... a bit," I replied. I didn't want to give her a big head.

"I bet you'd like me if you got to know me," she said. "It's my lunch break now. We could go for a walk together."

I had a lot of shopping to do, but I felt sorry for her.

"All right," I said. "But I haven't got all day."

She smiled, switched off the green arrow above her window and then got down from her chair and came round to where I was standing. She was dressed smartly, like a newsreader, with a matching jacket and skirt and little pearl earrings. We walked out of the building society together.

"Where do you want to go?" she said.

"Well, I was going to do some shopping."

"I can help."

I said all right, and we crossed the road to the first shop on my list, Just Write, which sells stationery and pens.

"OK," I said as we went into the shop. "I need some pens and a pad of Basildon Bond writing paper with matching envelopes."

Without any directions from me, Karen rushed over to the pen rack, chose a selection of blue and black biros and then collected the paper and envelopes.

"Here you are," she said, handing me everything with a smile. "Anything else?"

"No, that's it," I said, and went over to the desk to pay.

After that we went to a little shop on the corner called Sock Shop and Karen helped me choose a dozen pairs of socks and a dozen pairs of pants. The pants were mainly striped and the socks had animals on them, like pigs and parrots.

Once I had paid, we left the shop and stood outside on the pavement.

"Don't you have to go back to work, now?" I said.

"I can take the rest of the day off if I want."

"But I don't have any more shopping to do," I said, looking at my list.

"Well, why don't we go for a walk by the river?" she said, smiling, and took hold of my hand.

We walked to the riverbank and when we got there, we stopped and looked across the water. I took my hand away from hers. She looked up, hurt.

"Why did you do that?" she said.

"Don't over-react," I replied. "My hand was just feeling a bit hot."

Her face brightened and we carried on looking out at the river. After a while, she spoke.

"Would you mind if I did some gymnastics?" she said.

I shook my head and then watched as she took a few steps back down the gravel path and began her run up. After a few strides she leapt forwards and placed her hands on the ground, springing into the air and landing on her feet.

"That's an Arab Spring," she said, turning towards me and smiling.

"You look a bit flushed now," I said. Her face was red.

"Yes," she replied. "Could we go back to your house to have a drink of water?"

"OK," I said, and we set off back to my house.

When we got home, I unlocked the door with my key and put down my bags in the hall. Karen went into the kitchen to pour herself a glass of water, and I followed. Then she turned to me.

"Thank you very much," she said. "This is the best date I've ever had. Would you like me to bake you a cake?"

I thought for a moment.

"What kind of cake?"

"A fruit cake – or a cream cake – or a chocolate cake. Any kind of cake."

"Chocolate cake."

I came closer and watched as she started to break eggs and put butter and powder and milk into a big china bowl, and then mixed it all up with a spatula. After she had done quite a lot of stirring, she poured it all out into a cake tin lined with grease-proof paper, and then put that in a pre-heated oven. Then she came over to me with the bowl and let me scrape up all the mixture that was left and lick the spatula, which I did while she watched.

While the cake baked, we played cards on the kitchen table and then we went outside into the garden and played a couple of games of Swingball, which I won easily with the help of my trainers. When we heard the oven go 'TING', we came back in and she made a pot of tea while I sliced the cake and then we ate it with our fingers and drank the tea.

"What other games do you have?" she said as I sipped my tea.

"Well... I have Scrabble, Cluedo, Stay Alive, Monopoly, Downfall, Risk, Twister, Totopoly and Yahtzee," I replied.

Just then the doorbell rang. I went to answer the door, and outside to my surprise were Claudia Carpenter, formerly of *Decisions, Decisions* and Ulrika Jonsson.

"Hello," said Claudia. "We were just passing through. Do you mind if we come in?"

I let them in and they followed me into the kitchen and I introduced them to Karen.

"Now we've got four people," said Karen. "Why don't we play Twister?"

"Yes, let's play Twister," said Ulrika.

"OK," I replied, "but let me finish my tea first."

When I had finished my tea, we went into the living room and I got out the Twister set from the toy box. I unfolded the game mat and set up the pointer as Karen took off her shoes. Then Claudia and Ulrika did the same. Karen said that she wanted to go first, and I flicked the pointer. It landed on red. Karen placed her toe on the nearest red spot on the mat. Then I flicked the pointer again for me. It came up blue.

"Why don't you take off your shoes?" said Claudia.

"Well... I like them. They're new."

"Yes, but you don't want to get them dirty, do you?" said Ulrika.

I could see that they had a point, and I took off my shoes. Then I put my foot down on a blue spot.

Claudia flicked the arrow. This time it came up yellow, and she leaned over and put her hand on a yellow dot right next to my foot. After that, Ulrika spun and placed her hand on a red dot over by Karen. Then Karen had a go, and put her other hand on a green dot right next to my hand.

"Your turn," she said.

I spun the arrow again. It came up yellow, and I decided to place my hand on a spot on the opposite corner of the mat.

"You can't get away from me that easily," Karen said, laughing.

Then we all had the rest of our goes in turn. Before long we had to start spinning the spinner with our toes, which was quite funny. We ended up all over each other. Karen's leg was over my shoulder and my foot was somewhere in the middle of Ulrika and Claudia.

"We've run out of hands and feet," said Ulrika. "I can't spin the spinner from here."

I thought for a moment.

"Why don't we just stay like this for a while?"

We all agreed, and held our positions for quite a long time, just managing to stay upright.

When we got tired, I untangled myself, put my shoes back on

and went out to get *Lambada Nights* from the video shop, while the girls dusted the whole house. Then we all squeezed together on the sofa and really enjoyed the film.

Yours truly,

Pierre Stone

PS: I would appreciate it if you sent back my presents as I would like to give Claudia the Travel Wet Pouch and Ulrika the Slumber Shades.

Dear Marie,

Today I went to Costcutter to buy a pint of milk. I got up as usual, but just before I went out I needed to go to the loo, so I went back upstairs, undid my trousers, pulled down my pants and sat down on the toilet seat. After a little bit of straining, I felt some poo emerge and drop into the toilet water. Then some more came out, and after I heard another splash, I took two squares of paper from the toilet roll, folded them over into double-thickness and wiped myself. Then I inspected the paper, dropped it into the toilet behind me and wiped my bottom a few more times until there was nothing left. After that I got up, pulled my clothes back on and flushed the toilet before leaving for the shop.

When I got there, I took the milk from the shop fridge and then had a look around to see if there was anything else I wanted. I chose a Twix bar, a Drifter and a Milky Way from the sweet rack, and also a packet of Nik-Naks, which I had never tried before. Then I turned round and had a look at the magazine rack. There was the new issue of *Radio Times*, and I picked up a copy. Then I scanned the rest of the rack to see if there were any magazines which might be interesting. After some thought I picked up the latest issues of *Autocar, Kerrang!, Horny Bitches* and *Homes And Gardens*.

I went over to the till and gave the man my stack of magazines as well as my sweets and crisps. While he checked the prices of everything, I turned round and pretended to be interested in the greeting cards that were on display. Then I paid the money that he asked for, got my change, picked up my stuff and left. I walked home quickly, and when I got inside I put all the magazines down on the coffee table in the living room, sat down on the settee and ate the Nik-Naks while I flicked through *Radio Times*. I checked that *Decisions, Decisions* was on as scheduled, and then I turned to the back page, Tom Baker's My Kind of Day. Tom

Baker says that he feels more real when playing Professor Hoyt in *Medics* than he does in everyday life.

After that I flicked through *Kerrang!*, which is about heavy metal bands like Motley Crue and Soundgarden. Then I had a look at *Autocar*, which I found quite boring, and *Homes And Gardens*, which was also quite boring, although there were nice pictures of some homes and some gardens. Once I'd put that down I picked up *Horny Bitches*. There was a girl on the front wearing just her underwear, with her finger in her mouth and her legs spread apart. After looking at her for a while, I opened it up. The first two pages were advertisements, and then page three and four were the index, with some pictures of what was inside.

Next there were some video reviews which I flicked through, and on page 22, I came to the letters page. The first letter was from a man whose name and address had been withheld on request. It is a true account of a series of events concerning his wife which would probably never have occurred if he had not encouraged her to share her fantasies with him. He says: "These events would probably never have occurred had I not encouraged her to share her fantasies. You have to be prepared for the consequences when you allow someone to turn fantasy into reality." He goes on to talk about her keen interest in tennis and the competitions she enters at their local tennis club. "She's the best-looking player at the club and gets a lot of male attention, especially her short white pleated skirts and brief white panties. The linesmen must look forward to the moment when she bends down to pick up a ball and gives a glimpse of her now damp panties which have become a mere thong."

He then talks about sex with her and what it is like. Sometimes when she is lying on her back he will use his finger and his tongue together. His finger explores her dripping gash while his tongue flicks at her clitoris. She likes it when he uses his lips and teeth to suck and nibble at her clit. Meanwhile his finger slides slowly in and out of her swollen and wet vulva. He sometimes uses three fingers inside her until his hand is totally covered in her juices as her pouting mound, which is quite extraordinarily wet by now, pulses with each wave of vaginal juices that gush out between her legs.

After that letter, there were two more advertisements, one for Dateline and one for a subscription to *Horny Bitches*, with a picture of a businessman sitting on a busy train, thinking: "No one knows I get *Horny Bitches* delivered through my door." Then there was a photo spread of 'Bitch of the Month', Cherry North. She's a gorgeous blonde with a knockout figure and a degree in Business Studies, but the combination of beauty and brains hasn't always worked in her favour. "I used to work as a financial consultant," she explains, "and some clients wouldn't believe someone with my looks was capable of handling their portfolios!" This horny bitch can handle our hard currency any time she likes, the magazine goes on to say.

After looking at a few more spreads of girls, including Carrie, Melissa, Catherine and Shannon, and a photo feature on the new Ford Cosworth, I felt my penis beginning to grow and I adjusted my trousers. The next page I turned to featured adverts for a super range of sex aids. First there was Miss World, full size with long silky hair. And Super Shirley – full size, long hair, vibrating action, soft skin, perfumed. Also on sale were: Silk Lips – strokes up and down your penis by itself. Sensational. Magic Power Ring – to help hold your erection for longer lasting satisfaction. Penisator – sensational vibes from this ring for orgasmic experience. Vibrating Egg – ultimate vaginal experience. Strong vibrations will give hours of pleasure. Gold Tip – 10" with gold head. Multi speed. Ultimate status symbol. Also the Vacuum Penis Exerciser for a better erection, and Rubber Bermudas with Penis Pouch in small, medium and large.

The next page was the Masturbation Express page, featuring European strength phone sex now available for the first time in the UK. I had a look through the different ones on offer, which included: Correction for your Erection, College Lesbians, Naked in the Bus Shelter, Screams of a Virgin, Warm Facial Fountain, New Nanny for Big Baby, Listen To Me Pee, I'll Use Your

Tongue As Toilet Paper, Sticky Knickers Shame, Office Potty, Older Women Doggy Style, Girl Obeys Science Master, White Panties Red Cheeks, Kiss My Knickers and Model Hitchhiker Cheeks Parted By Strict SS Lesbians.

By now my penis was so large that I had to undo my flies and help it out of my underpants. Then I decided to call one of the numbers on offer. I thought about dialling New Nanny for Big Baby, but after some deliberation I chose Girl Obeys Science Master. I picked up the phone and despite a slight shaking in my hand, dialled the number that was printed on the page. I pressed the receiver close to my ear, but I could hear nothing. Then, to my relief, I heard a 'Click' sound and a dialling tone. This rang several times before I heard another 'Click', and a voice appeared.

"Thank you for calling this very naughty phone line," said the girl on the other end, in a husky voice. "You are about to hear the strongest European phone sex, available in the UK for the very first time. We would like to remind callers that the material you are about to hear is of an explicitly sexual nature, suitable only for those over eighteen years of age. If you are under eighteen, or if you think you would be offended by very explicit material, please hang up now."

Since that description did not apply to me, I decided not to hang up. Instead I kept the receiver to my ear and listened as another voice came on the line.

"Thank you for calling," she said. "I'm Suzy, and in a few moments you will hear the specially recorded message. But just before that, I want to tell you about the special service we have on offer. Just after the message you are about to hear, I will come back on the phone and give you a number that you can ring to connect to a live callback. That's right - live, one-on-one chat with sexy girls who are just dying to hear from you. So, remember to get a pen and paper out to write down that special number, just after the upcoming message."

I was going to get a pen and paper as Suzy had suggested, but then I thought about it and decided that I didn't want a live callback. I waited and after a few seconds another voice came on the line.

"You are about to hear a very sexy message," she said. "But before we start, I should remind listeners that this service is for those over 18 only. If you are under 18, please hang up now. We are also obliged to remind callers that the cost of this service is 34 pee a minute off-peak, 45 pee a minute peak rate."

I was getting a little bit bored with all these introductory messages, and I could feel my penis going soft and shrinking. However, after a while I could hear some faint sounds of a girl moaning and groaning, and this made it become hard again. Then another voice came on the line.

"Hi there," she said. "My name is Liz, and I'm here to tell you all about what happened to me the other day. Are you sitting comfortably? Then I'll begin!"

Liz had a very nice voice, sort of breathy but at the same time quite cheerful. I could feel my penis getting harder and I started to rub the end of it as I held the phone to my ear with my shoulder.

"I live in a little village and there's never much to do when my husband goes out to work during the day. However, one of my favourite errands is going down to the butcher's shop, because there's a man who works behind the counter who I think is really hunky. His name is Bill. He's very tall and has got these big hairy arms which I often imagine being wrapped around me! Anyway, the other day I was going down to the butcher's to buy some food for dinner. Maybe I should describe myself a little bit. I'm quite petite, five foot four inches with long blonde hair. I have a figure which a lot of people compliment me on – big tits and a nice round bum. I often wear short skirts to show off my shapely legs and that day was no exception."

I was a little confused as to what this had to do with Girl Obeys Science Master, but I carried on listening anyway.

"As I walked down towards the butcher's shop, I was getting excited just thinking about Bill and his gorgeous hunky body. When I got to the shop, I went in and he was standing behind the counter. There was no one else in the shop and he looked quite bored, but his face lit up when he saw me.

'Hi Bill,' I said. 'How are you today?'

He said he was fine, and then asked me what I wanted to buy.

'I don't know', I said. 'What have you got?'

'Well, I've got these sausages', he said, pointing to a tray full of sausages in the glass cabinet.

'They're not sausages, they're chipolatas,' I said, giggling. 'They're tiny! Haven't you got anything bigger?'

'Well, I have got my own personal sausage. If you come into the back room with me I'll give you a taste of it.'

'Is it nice and juicy?' I asked.

'Oh yes. Biggest sausage in the village,' he replied.

'How big, exactly?' I said.

'Ooh... about seven inches – pure beef,' he said. 'More than enough to satisfy a girl like you.'

I couldn't refuse an offer like that, and I followed Bill into the back room. Once we were inside, he turned round and he was holding his sausage in his hand, squeezing it gently. It certainly was the biggest sausage I had ever seen. It was long and very thick. My mouth watered as I examined it. Then I reached down and held it lovingly in my hand, licking the end of it. I parted my lips and slowly pushed the sausage into my mouth, feeling its thickness. I tasted it with my tongue, and then moved it round my mouth until the juice spurted out and trickled down my chin.

After that, we went back into the main shop and I bought two pounds of chipolatas. I smiled naughtily at Bill as he gave me my change, and then I strolled home. I gave them to my husband for dinner that night – little did he know about my shopping trip!"

Then the message ended. I heard Suzy's voice come on the line a few seconds later, but I hung up before she could read out the number. I was confused and disappointed. Not only was there nothing to do with Girl Obeys Science Master, but while Liz had been going on and on about sausages, my penis had been shrinking steadily.

I wanted to listen to the real Girl Obeys Science Master story and thought of ringing again to see if it was there this time. But then I realized that the story probably never existed at all. It was just a name on a piece of paper made up as a lie to deceive honest people like me.

I felt tired and angry and after I zipped up my trousers, I went upstairs and wrote all this down to you.

Yours truly,

Pierre Stone

I'm sorry I'm sorry I'm sorry I'm sorry I'm sorry I'm sorry I'm
sorry I'm sorry I'm sorry I'm sorry I'm sorry I'm sorry I'm sorry
I'm sorry I'm sorry I'm sorry I'm sorry I'm sorry I'm sorry I'm
sorry I'm sorry I'm sorry I'm sorry I'm sorry I'm sorry I'm sorry
I'm sorry I'm sorry I'm sorry I'm sorry I'm sorry I'm sorry I'm
sorry I'm sorry I'm sorry I'm sorry I'm sorry I'm sorry I'm sorry
I'm sorry I'm sorry I'm sorry I'm sorry I'm sorry I'm sorry I'm
sorry I'm sorry I'm sorry I'm sorry I'm sorry I'm sorry I'm sorry
I'm sorry I'm sorry I'm sorry I'm sorry I'm sorry I'm sorry I'm
sorry I'm sorry I'm sorry I'm sorry I'm sorry I'm sorry I'm sorry
I'm sorry I'm sorry I'm sorry I'm sorry I'm sorry I'm sorry I'm
sorry I'm sorry I'm sorry I'm sorry I'm sorry I'm sorry I'm sorry
I'm sorry I'm sorry I'm sorry I'm sorry I'm sorry I'm sorry I'm
sorry I'm sorry I'm sorry I'm sorry I'm sorry I'm sorry I'm sorry
I'm sorry I'm sorry I'm sorry I'm sorry I'm sorry I'm sorry I'm
sorry I'm sorry I'm sorry I'm sorry I'm sorry I'm sorry I'm sorry
I'm sorry I'm sorry I'm sorry I'm sorry I'm sorry I'm sorry I'm
sorry I'm sorry I'm sorry I'm sorry I'm sorry I'm sorry I'm sorry
I'm sorry I'm sorry I'm sorry I'm sorry I'm sorry I'm sorry I'm
sorry I'm sorry I'm sorry I'm sorry I'm sorry I'm sorry I'm sorry
I'm sorry I'm sorry I'm sorry I'm sorry I'm sorry I'm sorry I'm
sorry I'm sorry I'm sorry I'm sorry I'm sorry I'm sorry I'm sorry
I'm sorry I'm sorry I'm sorry I'm sorry I'm sorry I'm sorry I'm
sorry I'm sorry I'm sorry I'm sorry I'm sorry I'm sorry I'm sorry
I'm sorry I'm sorry I'm sorry I'm sorry I'm sorry I'm sorry I'm
sorry I'm sorry I'm sorry I'm sorry I'm sorry I'm sorry I'm sorry
I'm sorry I'm sorry I'm sorry I'm sorry I'm sorry I'm sorry I'm
sorry I'm sorry I'm sorry I'm sorry I'm sorry I'm sorry I'm sorry
I'm sorry I'm sorry I'm sorry I'm sorry I'm sorry I'm sorry I'm
sorry I'm sorry I'm sorry I'm sorry I'm sorry I'm sorry I'm sorry

I must not talk about disgusting things.
I must not talk about disgusting things.
I must not talk about disgusting things.
I must not talk about disgusting things.
I must not talk about disgusting things.
I must not talk about disgusting things.
I must not talk about disgusting things.
I must not talk about disgusting things.
I must not talk about disgusting things.
I must not talk about disgusting things.
I must not talk about disgusting things.
I must not talk about disgusting things.
I must not talk about disgusting things.
I must not talk about disgusting things.
I must not talk about disgusting things.
I must not talk about disgusting things.
I must not talk about disgusting things.
I must not talk about disgusting things.
I must not talk about disgusting things.
I must not talk about disgusting things.
I must not talk about disgusting things.
I must not talk about disgusting things.
I must not talk about disgusting things.
I must not talk about disgusting things.
I must not talk about disgusting things.
I must not talk about disgusting things.
I must not talk about disgusting things.
I must not talk about disgusting things.
I must not talk about disgusting things.
I must not talk about disgusting things.
I must not talk about disgusting things.
I must not talk about disgusting things.
I must not talk about disgusting things.
I must not talk about disgusting things.
I must not talk about disgusting things.
I must not talk about disgusting things.
I must not talk about disgusting things.
I must not talk about disgusting things.
I must not talk about disgusting things.

I must not make things up.
I must not make things up.
I must not make things up.
I must not make things up.
I must not make things up.
I must not make things up.
I must not make things up.
I must not make things up.
I must not make things up.
I must not make things up.
I must not make things up.
I must not make things up.
I must not make things up.
I must not make things up.
I must not make things up.
I must not make things up.
I must not make things up.
I must not make things up.
I must not make things up.
I must not make things up.
I must not make things up.
I must not make things up.
I must not make things up.
I must not make things up.
I must not make things up.
I must not make things up.
I must not make things up.
I must not make things up.
I must not make things up.
I must not make things up.
I must not make things up.
I must not make things up.
I must not make things up.
I must not make things up.
I must not make things up.
I must not make things up.

Science Master obeys Girl.
Science Master obeys Girl.
Science Master obeys Girl.
Science Master obeys Girl.
Science Master obeys Girl.
Science Master obeys Girl.
Science Master obeys Girl.
Science Master obeys Girl.
Science Master obeys Girl.
Science Master obeys Girl.
Science Master obeys Girl.
Science Master obeys Girl.
Science Master obeys Girl.
Science Master obeys Girl.
Science Master obeys Girl.
Science Master obeys Girl.
Science Master obeys Girl.
Science Master obeys Girl.
Science Master obeys Girl.
Science Master obeys Girl.
Science Master obeys Girl.
Science Master obeys Girl.
Science Master obeys Girl.
Science Master obeys Girl.
Science Master obeys Girl.
Science Master obeys Girl.
Science Master obeys Girl.
Science Master obeys Girl.
Science Master obeys Girl.
Science Master obeys Girl.
Science Master obeys Girl.
Science Master obeys Girl.
Science Master obeys Girl.
Science Master obeys Girl.
Science Master obeys Girl.
Science Master obeys Girl.
Science Master obeys Girl.

Dear Marie,

You may have received a letter signed by Pierre Stone and dated the 18th of November.

Even though it was signed by Pierre Stone, it wasn't written by Pierre Stone, but by an impostor who burgled into this house and stole my pen and copied my handwriting.

I will let you know how the police get on with the case. Rest assured that any further letters you receive will be definitely from me, as the pen he stole was very low on ink and he only took a small amount of paper.

Many apologies for this inconvenience.

Yours truly,

Pierre Stone

Dear Marie,

People don't understand how great you are. They see you on the television and read about your lifestyle, but they don't realize. You are nothing like the others. *They Cannot Touch You.*

You are like the Good Witch of the East, but more so. Without you, life on this planet would not be worth living. Other people are worse than scum in a kettle compared to you.

Yours truly,

Pierre Stone

PS: All your other so-called fans aren't really fans.

Dear Marie,

There is something going on which is very important that you know about. I have considered calling the police but have held back for your sake.

Tony Clayton is stalking me. He has been hiding behind trees and lampposts and watching me as I go to the shops. I believe he is taking notes about my movements although I can't see his notebooks so probably they are mental notes.

He knows I have spotted him so he has taken to disguising himself as a Frenchman, complete with beret and onions. At first I thought this couldn't be Tony Clayton, but then I remembered he wore the exact same outfit in a sketch on the show last September. You were a waitress in a French café and it ended with you singing a song together.

Yesterday he cycled alongside me the whole way as I went to the building society. I pretended not to notice him, but I knew he was there, he knew that I knew, and I knew he knew I knew.

I came out of the building society to find him leaning on his bicycle, eyeing me and chomping an onion. I knew he wasn't enjoying it, he was only doing it so I would think he was hard.

When I got home he was waiting across the road. He must have cycled back double-quick to beat me, but he didn't look sweaty. He stared at me, smiled and gave me his trademark wink, but it didn't seem like a friendly wink, it seemed like a menacing wink.

Just before I went to bed, I heard a 'thump' on the front door. I opened it and there was no one there but I looked down to see an onion lying on the doorstep.

Yours defiantly,

Pierre Stone

Dear Marie,

This morning I awoke to find a letter on the hall carpet. It was addressed to me and signed by Tony Clayton.

When I read the letter, I was shocked, horrified and upset. It's not something I would normally show you but I think it's important. Please find the letter enclosed. I think it speaks for itself.

Yours, shocked, horrified and upset,

Pierre Stone

Dear Mr Stone,

I don't know what the FUCK you think you are
doing but it's gone on long enough.

Your letters to my assistant are ruining
everything. She has become a different woman
since receiving them. All she talks about is
you and I hate this. She doesn't know I have
been intercepting her replies all along and you
better fucking not tell her. If you ever try
to see her in person or whisk her away to
a better life I will kill you.

I know she has been thinking about leaving the
show and I put this down to your influence.
Before she met you she was perfectly happy
doing what she was told but now she's full of
ideas.

I'm in love with her and I will do anything
to stop someone like you getting hold of her.
She's the most beautiful woman in the world and
she doesn't think anything for me and I'm dying
inside. At the moment she won't even give me
the time of day.

However, I get to be around her all day and
you don't. Even though you're so-called best
friends, you've never actually met!

We share a changing room, and I get to watch
her get changed. I saw her getting changed
the other day and it was great. She had on
a lovely bra and pants. Then she took them off
and I could see her xxxx and xxxx close-up.

She bent over to pick something up and I could
see right up her xxxx. It was all moist
I wanted to take a xxx xxxxx and xxxxx xx xxxx

xx xxx.

If I could I'd put it in her contract that
she'd have to sit on my face. I've got
a picture of her I cut from a magazine and
I stick it over my pillow at night and xxxxx xx
xxxx xx xx xxxxx xxx xxxxx xx and imagine it's
really her. That does me for a while but then
I see her the next day and it starts all over
again, I just want to bang her. I'd do it up
against the wall if she'd let me. I'd do it
in the xxxxx with her xxxx in the xxxx if
I wasn't scared of the police. I'd do it
everywhere, all the time if I could.

I'd do it live on TV while the stupid
fucking contestants are making up their minds
with her bent over the Quizboard. I'd tell the
cameras to keep rolling so it would go through
the News.

If she had a baby I wouldn't look after it,
I'd probably leave that to someone stupid
like you.

Of course, none of this is going to happen.
Because she doesn't love me or even fancy me.
Soon the frustration is going to get too much
and I'll do something I'll live to regret.

Yours angrily,

TONY CLAYTON

Dear Marie,

When you came on tonight, I knew there was something different in the way you looked at me as you crossed the stage.

"I had a nightmare last night, Tony," you said.

Tony made a joke and the audience laughed.

"I was being chased by this horrible creature – so horrible it defies description – and as it was chasing me, I could feel it breathing down my neck. It was really horrible, and I was very frightened, but no matter how fast I was running it seemed to be gaining on me."

You paused and Tony listened expectantly.

"It was right behind me, and it was just about to get me when a handsome young hunter appeared to rescue me. He was carrying a bow and arrow and quick as a flash he fired three shots."

"And did he kill the monster?"

"No – you escaped Tony!"

Then the audience laughed and clapped but when you started smiling at the camera, I could tell that your dream was a message.

Thank you.

Yours forever,

Pierre Stone

Dear Marie,

This afternoon Pierre Stone got ready to leave his house. He ate a peanut butter and chocolate spread sandwich, had a shower, shaved, and combed his hair. Then he got changed into his grey Top Man trousers, his new Reebok Trek Off Road HXL trainers and his Global Hypercolour T-shirt. Before he left the house he remembered to clean his teeth and have a last pee. Then he put on his dark green jacket and left through the front door.

As he walked down the street, Pierre Stone fingered the tickets in his hand and thought about where he was going, which made him walk faster. It was quite a long walk to Purley Station, so to make it shorter he went through the cemetery. He looked at the names on the gravestones to see if he could see his father's name, but he couldn't find it. He didn't even know if his father was buried there, but he looked just in case.

After maybe ten or fifteen minutes he arrived at the station. There was a man behind the ticket window, but he decided to use the ticket machine instead, and got out a handful of change from his trouser pocket. First he pressed the button marked 'London Underground Zone 123456', then the button marked 'Adult Single', then put in the exact change and listened as the machine printed his ticket.

While he was waiting on the platform, Pierre Stone looked up to see where the train should be coming from, but there was nothing there, just railway tracks going off into a vanishing point. He looked at the vanishing point for what seemed like a very long time. Then he heard a sound, followed by the sight of a far-off train which slowly became bigger as it approached the station.

When the train came to a halt, Pierre Stone approached the nearest door, pressed the black rubber button and stepped in. He considered pretending it was one of the Moonbase Alpha trains from *Space: 1999*, but decided against it. Instead, he just sat down on a seat which was furthest away from the nearest person.

The train stopped at Purley Oaks, South Croydon, East Croydon, Selhurst, Thornton Heath, Norbury, Streatham Common, Balham, Wandsworth Common, Clapham Junction, Queenstown Road and Vauxhall before coming to rest at Waterloo. Pierre Stone stood up, pressed the button marked Open and walked down the platform. He showed his ticket to the man at the barrier, who clearly didn't suspect a thing. Then he followed the signs for the Underground.

After navigating two escalators and an automatic gate, he arrived on the platform for the Northbound Northern Line. Before long a train arrived and he got on, sat down, gripped the armrests and contemplated his fate. The train went through Westminster, Charing Cross and Leicester Square. Getting off at Tottenham Court Road, Pierre Stone looked to find a sign for the Central Line, which was the one he needed to get to White City. Because the sign was in red it didn't take him long to find it.

He followed the arrows down a series of tunnels until he came to another, different platform. This one had a computer screen which said "West Ruislip, 2 mins/Ealing Broadway 5 mins." While he was waiting, Pierre Stone noticed a vending machine behind him, and he put in some money. Normally he would have chosen chocolate, such as Dairy Milk or Fruit and Nut, but because this was a serious day and he was trying to be serious, he pressed the button for Wrigley's Spearmint chewing gum instead.

The train arrived and he got on, chewing the gum as he went through Oxford Circus, Bond Street, Marble Arch, Lancaster Gate, Queensway, Notting Hill Gate, Holland Park, Shepherd's Bush and White City. When he arrived at White City, he went to one of the gate machines and put his ticket into the slot. The ticket disappeared and the gate opened, allowing him through. Once at the exit he went up to a man wearing a London Undergound hat and asked him the way to the television centre.

"Just turn left, and it's on your right," he said. "You can't miss it."

Pierre Stone thanked the man and walked out of the station.

Before long the television centre came into sight and he crossed the road towards the gate. There was a main gate for vehicles and a smaller one for pedestrians. Putting his hands inside his coat pockets, he went up to the smaller gate. There was a man in the sentry box with a white beard.

"I've come to see *Decisions, Decisions* starring Tony Clayton," he said.

"Can I see your ticket, sir?" said the sentry.

He handed the man his ticket. After a brief inspection, it was given back to him.

"Can you tell me where to go?" he said.

"Just go over to that main door," said the man, pointing to a door beneath a green roof. "Ask at reception, they'll tell you the way to the studio."

Pierre Stone did as he had been told, and went over through the glass doors. Once inside, he went to talk to another uniformed man behind a desk.

"I've come to see *Decisions, Decisions* starring Tony Clayton," he said.

"Right, just go through those double doors on your right, walk all the way down, turn left at the end and then follow signs to Studio 7."

He thanked the man and followed the directions that he had been given. On the way, he saw Maggie Philbin coming through a door, but he didn't stop. When he got to the room marked Studio 7, he found that there was a long queue outside it. He thought for a moment and then joined it. The queue consisted mainly of old people and people with loud voices who he didn't want to speak to. When he got to the door, a woman inspected his ticket and let him inside.

The studio was very big. There were rows and rows of seats stretching back towards the ceiling. There was a railing and then there were a lot of cameras and other equipment, and then there was the stage. The stage was big and empty, with electric lights around the edges just like on television. Pierre Stone went up to the fourth row, and sat on the seat nearest the aisle. People kept pushing past him to get to seats further down, but he did his best to ignore them.

Before long, the only empty seat in his row was the one right next to him. Then he saw two old women come slowly up the aisle. When they got to the fourth row, they stopped.

"Excuse me young man, but would you mind moving so that my friend and I can sit in those seats?" one of them said.

"Why?" he said. "I got here first."

"It's just that the only other seats are quite a long way up, you know."

He frowned.

"Well – I suppose so."

Pierre Stone reluctantly got up and walked up the stairs, towards the back of the studio. There weren't any other aisle seats left, in fact the only one he could find was three seats in, second row from the back. He squeezed past three fat people, sat down in his seat and folded his arms.

He waited for what seemed like a very long time, trying not to listen to all the stupid conversations going on around him. Then everybody was quiet because a man wearing glasses and holding a clipboard came up to the front of the stage. He welcomed them all to the show, and then he asked them to show him how loud they could clap. They all clapped, and then he said, "That's not good enough!" and they did it again, louder. Then he showed them a big card saying "Applause" which he said they should watch out for during the show.

After that, another man with a microphone came on. He came closer than the first man, right up to the front row. He announced himself, but Pierre Stone didn't know his face and he had never heard his name. He started telling jokes which a lot of people laughed at, but Pierre Stone didn't find them funny. He went up to a man in the audience and made a joke about his bald head which everyone laughed at. He went right up the aisle to the back and then down the other aisle, telling jokes and picking on people. Everyone seemed to think he was funny, but he wasn't.

When he left there was silence as the man with glasses came on again, to announce that the show would soon be starting. There was quite a bit of activity round by the cameras as everyone got to their places. Then everyone stopped moving. All of a sudden Tony Clayton came bounding out from the back of the set towards the audience. Everyone started clapping except Pierre Stone. He put his hand inside his pocket and fingered his father's army pistol which he'd remembered to bring from the box in the loft. Everyone was clapping and cheering loudly. Pierre Stone got out of his seat and pushed past the people sitting next to him.

He got to the aisle and the cheers were still so loud that he could creep all the way down the stairs without being noticed. When he got to the bottom, he caught the eye of the man with glasses, but then he quickly turned away. Just then the clapping began to subside.

"Welcome to *Decisions, Decisions!*" said Tony.

Pierre Stone pulled his father's gun from his pocket, pushed the catch down and climbed over the railings. He started to run towards the stage. The man with glasses started running after him.

"The show where earning your bread..."

Pierre Stone pointed the gun at Tony Clayton.

"... means using your head."

Pierre Stone pulled the trigger. At the same moment he felt himself trip over one of the cables on the floor. The gun went off with a very loud bang and there was a flash as some lights burst on the stage. Then the gun flew out of his hand. There was a lot of screaming and shouting and there were a lot of people on top of Pierre Stone. He struggled for a while but then he gave up and they dragged him out of the studio.

Some of the men who were holding Pierre Stone shouted at him and said rude things to him. They took him into an office and held him down on a chair, then they stood him up and took him outside. There was a police car waiting outside with some policemen in it. One of the policemen put Pierre Stone's arms behind his back and put handcuffs on him. Then he put him in the back seat of the car. They said some things to him about his rights and then when they got to the police station they put him in a cell. Then they took him out of that and put him in another room with a table and chairs. They asked him what he had done and why, and he told them. After a while, they put him back in his cell and took off his handcuffs and Pierre Stone took a pencil from his pocket and wrote this to you on the wall.

Yours truly,

Pierre Stone

Dear Marie,

You may find this handwriting familiar. Yes, it's your old friend, Pierre Stone. We haven't been in contact for a long time and you may have thought I had forgotten about you. Not true. In fact, I have simply been very busy and my schedule hasn't allowed time for letter-writing. No doubt you can relate to this.

Since my last update, I have been living in a new environment and have had a lot of new experiences, some good and some not so good. All in all, it has helped me to realise that the person I was is not the person I really am. There is a much bigger person with clearer ideas lurking inside me trying to get out, and at present he is succeeding.

To sum up, I have moved on considerably from when I was with you. It's not that I think that what we had together was a waste of time. It was OK for then. But now I have moved on, to the point that a relationship with you could no longer satisfy me.

I hope you don't take this too hard. I know the past year has been difficult for you and, of course, I will be there for you as a friend whenever you need me. Just drop me a line and I will be there. But the simple truth is that we were never meant for each other and it's time for us both to move on. I hope you don't mind that I've started first.

I wish you all the best with your career. I was sorry to hear that you had been replaced on *Decisions, Decisions* by Andrea Cole. If things keep not going well for you in television, you could always consider a less stressful career, like bakery.

I am returning the photo you sent me as I feel it would be inappropriate for me to keep hold of it. I hope you don't take this the wrong way.

Good wishes.

Yours truly,

Pierre Stone

PS: Please give my best to Claudia Carpenter.

ALSO AVAILABLE ON I.M.P. FICTION

THE PEACOCK MANIFESTO
by Stuart David

Peacock Johnson's got an idea. A masterplan to help him escape his criminal past. But he needs someone who can turn ideas into something real, so he's taking his idea to America.

Join him on the craziest journey of your life, but a word of warning, don't fuck with Glasgow's own Rhinestone Cowboy, because nothing is going to stand in his way. Not the nagging of his mad missus, Bev, nor the weird antics of his Yankee sidekick, Evil Bob.

As Peacock careers from one crisis to another, his aspirations and plans spiral out of control in a frenzy of hilarity, disaster, sadness and insanity. But this is America, the land of dreams, where anything is possible, even The Peacock Manifesto...or is it?

The Peacock Manifesto weaves farce with danger, splicing sensitive undercurrents with brutal reality, sucking the reader into Peacock's well-dressed, badly advised and always utterly compulsive world.

"Run out at once and buy David's darkly hilarious second novel."
Dazed & Confused

"Fast and funny." *The Guardian*

"A riotous second novel. Pure fucking genius." *Uncut* - 5★

"A fantastic second outing for David, proving the author's continuing skills, as a fine comic writer." *ID* Magazine

ISBN: 0-9533275-5-8   Paperback, 160 pages Price: £7.99
Web. www.peacock-johnson.com

THE BAD BOOK
by Stephen Jones

Hit had been happy as an eight year old. He didn't want to grow up. He was a sweet kid, but one that wasn't quite right. He had juvenile insomnia. He was somewhere floating between ME and E-Number hyperactivity. Even the weird bulge under his eye didn't seem to worry him. He was just happy to fall off the edge of the world and get up again. But then his mother goes missing, and all of a sudden he has to be an adult.

This striking debut novel documents a pivotal two days in Hit's bizarre life. It is a desperate, and disturbing tale of one boy's fight to win back a normal life. To find his lost mother and keep tabs on his father, the man he suddenly realises he knows nothing about.

Stephen Jones is the musical blacksheep Babybird. *The Bad Book* is Stephen's first novel, and has nothing to do with music whatsoever.

"Astonishing. *The Bad Book* shares its grotesque childlike detail with Ian Banks' *The Wasp Factory*, but the bleak surreality and contorted memory sequences belong to Jones." *The Times*

"It is breathtaking in its simplicity and its originality. Jones simply has a gift for the sort of words you relish wrapping your tongue around." *The Scotsman*

"Cryptic, yet this cossetted, wounded loner in dystopia will come back to haunt you... 'til infinity." *ID* Magazine

ISBN: 0-9533275-3-1   Paperback, 124 pages   Price: £6.99
Web: www.babybird.co.uk

NALDA SAID
by Stuart David

Riddled by an intense fear of his bizarre secret being discovered, the narrator of *Nalda Said* grows up in the strange seclusion of a shoddy caravan with his Aunt Nalda, whose own colourful storytelling leaves him perpetually trapped between fantasy and reality.

Nalda's nephew eventually finds work as a hospital gardener where, perhaps for the first time, he finds true friendship and begins to realise that his dark secret has been suffocating what hope he had of ever leading a normal life.

Finding himself in love, this socially disjointed figure struggles to reconcile his own curious view of the world with the stark daily reality that most people are forced to live with. *Nalda Said* is a compelling and brilliantly crafted tale of one man's pained anxiety and desperate search for his dream – to live a normal life.

"Delicately written and achingly sad, with just a hint of a moral in the poignant denouement, if David ever gives up the day job, pop music's loss could well be literature's gain." *The Times*

"Dark undercurrents of dread and skillful thriller rush... There's an echo of Salinger in *Nalda Said*'s dissection of alienation." *NME*

"Beguiling and ever so slightly unsettling, this is the insular terrain of *The Wasp Factory* and *The Butcher Boy* compassionately revisited." *The Face*

ISBN: 0-9533275-2-3 Paperback, 160 pages   Price: £7.99
Web: www.geometrid.co.uk

MILK, SULPHATE AND ALBY STARVATION
by Martin Millar

"What's allergic to milk, collects comics, sells speed, likes The Fall and lives in Brixton? Alby Starvation, the first true British anti-hero of the giro generation. Milk, Sulphate and Alby Starvation *is a strange and wonderful story of unbelievable allergies, seedy gutter violence and manic paranoia. I've yet to meet someone who has not enjoyed it."* NME

Your doctor refuses to believe you're allergic to just about everything, especially milk, there's a megalomaniac professor digging a hole outside your flat, your small stake in the amphetamine market in Brixton is being threatened by a mysterious Chinese man and the Milk Marketing Board have taken out a contract on your life. Welcome to the bizarre, obsessive world of Alby Starvation.

A world full of shop-lifting, death-threats, paranoia and video game arcades. Alby's frantic struggle to avoid being shot provides the hilarious and engaging back-drop for this, Martin Millar's debut novel.

"A welcome re-issue. This entertaining fable, which is alternately surreal and grubbily realistic, still delights." *The Times*

"Pop cultural references are everywhere in this frantic cultish debut which takes an Irvine Welsh-esque turn." *The Guardian*

"A masterful work that goes straight to the heart of a spurned generation. A work of rare genius and truly cult, it deserves a place on your book shelf next to Hubert Selby Jr's *Last Exit To Brooklyn*."

The List

"A minor classic... strange, quirky and entertaining to the end."

What's On London

ISBN: 0-9533275-4-X Paperback, 160 pages   Price £6.99
Web: www.martinmillar.com

THE TECHNO-PAGAN OCTOPUS MESSIAH
by Ian Winn

Part bizarre quest, part unique travelogue, part insane fiction, *The Techno-Pagan Octopus Messiah* is an extraordinary tale of prophetic dreams and adventurous treks through Egypt, Rajastan and northern India.

Winn disguises himself as a tourist and, catalysed by drugs from the Amazonian rain forest, takes the reader on a kaleidoscopic trip to places where crystals are dragon eggs, free love is expensive and tourist massacres mean discount hotels. Along the way lies among other things, a tantric commune, an illegal hike up the Pyramid of Chepren, and cryptic encounters with Indian snake saddhus.

Ian Winn is a leading star of the spoken-word circuit. His volatile performances have won high acclaim across both Britain and the USA.

"If you are looking for something a bit different this year, try Ian Winn's debut novel. It has all the travel fiction requisites in spades. Delivered with crazed enthusiasm and humour, it makes a refreshing change from the usual backpackers novels." *The Times*

"Inventive, brilliantly realised characters... displays a rampant thirst for mysticism and self-discovery. One can not help being won over by Winn's enthusiasm and intellectual energy." *The Sunday Times*

"The most progressive, alternative life-style novel of the decade." *Dream Creation*

"One astonishing book!" *Select*

ISBN: 0 9533275 1 5   Paperback, 288 pages   Price: £7.99
Web: www.octopusmessiah.com

LOVE AND PEACE WITH MELODY PARADISE
by Martin Millar

This is the story of Melody Paradise. You'll like her – everybody does. Women aspire to be like her and men fall in love with her. Melody is kind, spiritual and very beautiful. She's also on a mission... and nothing is going to stand in her way.

The travelling community to which she belongs has become horribly fragmented by a series of mysterious and chaotic happenings. Her mission is to reunite them. She organises a festival as the perfect vehicle to bring them together, during which an amazing story unfolds, often funny, sometimes sad, always compelling... and with a twist in the tail.

Through the words and eyes of Martin Millar, the reluctant guest novelist at Melody's festival, we become privileged observers of a world most of us would struggle to even imagine.

Martin Millar – Glaswegian hero to the post-punk generation, low-life socialite, pessimistic optimist, and incurable romantic. Also author of a host of cult classics including *Milk, Sulphate & Alby Starvation*, and *The Good Fairies of New York*.

"Brixton's answer to Kurt Vonnegut." *The Guardian*

"A charming tale... very funny." *Melody Maker*

"Hilarious and endearing comedy." *Scotland on Sunday*

ISBN: 0-9533275-0-7 Paperback, 288 pages   Price £6.99
Web: www.martinmillar.com

HOW TO ORDER:

Visit us at:

www.impbooks.com

for more information on titles, reviews,
author biographies and our music book label,
Independent Music Press, home to titles on
Stereophonics, Travis, Prodigy, David Bowie,
Beastie Boys, Shaun Ryder and more.

For any queries or for a free catalogue,
e-mail us at: info@impbooks.com

TO PURCHASE BY POST

Please make cheques/postal orders or
international money orders payable in £Sterling to:
I.M.P. FICTION LTD
and send your payment to:

I. M. P. FICTION (PS)
P.O. BOX 14691,
LONDON SE1 2ZA

Please allow 21 days for delivery.
Postage and packing is FREE in the UK,
£1.50 for Europe and £3.00 for the Rest of the World.